The Ultimate GIRLS' Guide to
SCIENCE

From Backyard Experiments to Winning the Nobel Prize!

by Beth Caldwell Hoyt & Erica Ritter

BEYOND

Table of Contents

The Ultimate GIRLS' Guide to
SCIENCE

Published by
Beyond Words Publishing, Inc.
20827 NW Cornell Road, Suite 500
Hillsboro, Oregon 97124
503-531-8700

Every effort has been made to contact the copyright owners of the photographs in this book. If the copyright holder of a photograph in this book has not heard from us, please contact Beyond Words Publishing. The publisher gratefully acknowledges and thanks the following for their generous assistance and permission to use photos:

Rachel Carson by Brooks Studio, Courtesy of the Lear/Carson Collection, Connecticut College
Mae Jemison, Photograph Courtesy of NASA
Margaret Knight Illustration Copyright © 2000 by Jerry McCann

Printed in the United States of America
Distributed to the book trade by Publishers Group West

Library of Congress Cataloging-in-Publication Data

Hoyt, Beth.
   The ultimate girls' guide to science : from backyard experiments to winning the Nobel
Prize! / written by Beth Hoyt and Erica Ritter.
      p. cm.
   Summary: Introduces scientific disciplines, profiles famous women scientists throughout history, provides directions for experiments, and presents quotations and resources to inspire further study.
      ISBN: 1-58270-092-3
      1. Science—Vocational guidance—Juvenile literature. 2. Women in science—Juvenile literature. [1. Science—Vocational guidance. 2. Vocational guidance. 3. Women in science.] I. Ritter, Erica. II. Title.

Q147.H69 2003
500'.82—dc21
2003041946

The corporate mission of Beyond Words Publishing, Inc.:
Inspire to Integrity

Science Is a "Girl Thing"

Do you gaze at the stars, searching for patterns in the sky? Do you like to take care of animals, trying to help them heal when they're hurt? How about gardening or watching wildlife? Do you enjoy experimenting in the kitchen with food concoctions? Though it may not seem so, all these activities involve science. That's the best part of science—it relates to everything we do and experience.

You may already be in love with science. If so, you'll be excited to find that you're in good company. History is filled with girls like you—girls who changed the world by studying science and solving problems. In this book you'll find remarkable women role models, and fellow young scientists who share your passion. You'll also find new directions to explore, and some ideas for getting your friends hooked on science, too!

Every day you learn about science during school. You do science homework and you take science tests. So why read a book about science in your free time? Because you know, like we do, that there's more to science than what's in a textbook. Science is more than worksheets and memorizing—it's exploring, discovering, thinking about the world, and satisfying your curiosity when nobody else has the answers.

We're lucky because women in the United States have the right to equal opportunities in science and education. Yet girls don't often choose careers in science, at least not as often as boys do. Sometime during their middle school years, many girls lose interest, or stop believing in their own abilities. Without encouragement, it is easy to give up—and miss the chance to discover all that science has to offer.

Science can be an exciting hobby, an awesome career, and a source of knowledge that you can use to pursue your dreams in any direction. Whatever your reasons for trying science, this guide will help you explore—and have fun in the process!

Chapter 1

Science: It's All Around You

Are you amazed by the patterns in everyday things: the way bubbles form in soapy water, how flags flap in the breeze, the timing of the best sunsets? Do you wonder what makes the world the way it is? You know in your heart that there is only one way to discover the answers you're after: SCIENCE!

Science isn't just a subject you study—it's a way of looking at the world. If you're curious about the "real" world—the world you can see, hear, touch, and explore—and want to know more about how things work and why things happen, you might be a budding scientist and not even know it. Science is behind everything we do. Every day, you are using your own hidden scientific skills to make discoveries about the world in which you live. Science is about curiosity and creativity. If you have these qualities, you have the makings of a great scientist.

Adventurous Women

Science is an adventure—some of the greatest women explorers in history were scientists. Maria Sibylla Merian started drawing butterflies and insects as a ten-year-old girl in Denmark, and soon began publishing books of her nature paintings. Her beautiful depictions of flowers and insects were used by scientists all over the world. Adventure draws modern scientists to explore, too—Jane Goodall, Dian Fossey, and many other researchers spent years in the wilderness hoping to discover the secrets of wild chimpanzees, mountain gorillas, or rare healing plants. Mexican biologist Claudia Padilla dove in a submersible—a small vessel for viewing sea life—hundreds of feet underwater to research black coral in the Yucatan.

Transforming the place where you live can be a great way to start an adventure. Betty Galloway invented a bubble-making machine when she was ten years old. Two sisters, Teresa and Mary Thompson, patented their solar Wigwam tent in 1960. Becky Schroeder invented a special glow-in-the-dark paper—the Glo-Sheet—when she was twelve, and eventually started her own company, B.J. Products Inc. The paper is used by police, emergency workers, and the U.S. government. One thing that all these adventurers had in common was their desire to continue questioning their experiences—to come up with new ways to look at the world, test their ideas, and add to our understanding of the world.

Is That Really Science?

You've probably heard of earth science, life science, and physical science. But food science? Domestic science? There are no limits to the number of different sciences; it's all about finding out what you want to know.

Some sciences are based on subjects that a lot of people find interesting or entertaining—the science of sound and music is called acoustics, for example, and the science of light is optics. "People watchers" might consider studying the social sciences of sociology or behavioral psychology. There's even a science of fireworks, called pyrotechnics. You can have a science dedicated to any topic—it just has to be something that other people can study, using the scientific method.

Applied Sciences: Some sciences focus on how we get the things we need: food, water, shelter, health care, or money, for example. Agricultural science, nutrition and food science, engineering, pharmacology and medicine, and economics are some of these. They're often called "applied sciences" because they're about applying science to everyday life.

Social Sciences: Some sciences help people to figure out mysteries about people: how people lived long ago, how a crime was committed, why people behave the way they do, what it means to be human. Archaeology, forensics, psychology, and anthropology are among these social sciences. History, geography, politics, and philosophy can also be studied scientifically, but some people don't count these as sciences.

Natural Sciences: What most people mean by "science" is studying things just for the sake of knowing about them. We call this "natural science." It's the study of the physical universe, and all its parts. Natural sciences include physics, chemistry, biology, medical research, ecology, geology, astronomy, and many other specialties. Natural scientists are usually looking for knowledge of how things work, not for a practical use in every day life. They are out to find the answers to questions like "How many stars are there?" and "What happens when you mix two chemicals together?" But some of the things they find—like electricity and genetics—become useful pretty fast!

Science Skills

When you think of science skills, what comes to mind? Maybe doing math, or graphing, or knowing big technical words, or working with microscopes, computers, or test tubes. These are all part of science, but they're just the tools. Some of the most important skills in science are personal characteristics: curiosity, patience, creativity, logic, cooperation, openness to new ideas, persistence, good judgment, and common sense. Scientists have to do their own work, make sure it's reliable, and that their experiments are repeatable. They have to listen to other people, and be the first to admit it if they're wrong.

How do scientists make great discoveries? Successful science means working hard, getting lucky, and having the skills and knowledge to use your luck.

Quiz—Is Science for You?

Were you the kind of young girl who always asked, "Why is the sky blue?" or "What happens to the light in the refrigerator when you close the door?" and even now find that the questions never stop? Take this quiz and find out if you are a scientist in the making.

1. When the teacher starts lecturing about black holes, you:
a) wonder how a black hole forms in the first place.
b) wish your arch-nemesis would get sucked into one.
c) start thinking about that episode of *Star Trek* where the crew gets sucked into a wormhole.

2. When you present your science fair project to the judges, you:
a) demonstrate how human digestion works by stuffing a piece of pepperoni pizza in your mouth.
b) articulate the hypothesis, method, data, and results of your experiment and receive a standing ovation.
c) find yourself staring at your crush, whose experiment is right next to yours.

3. When the radio dies in the middle of your favorite song, you:
a) yell for your brother to come and fix this piece of junk.
b) grab hold of the antenna with one hand, raise your arm in the air, and stand on one foot to try to get better reception.
c) unplug it and start taking it apart to see if you can figure out why it's not working.

4. Your mom wants you to help plant flowers in the garden. You:
a) examine the dirt, worms, and bugs you find as you are digging holes for the bulbs.
b) wish a bird would swoop down and eat some of the bugs and worms in your yard so you can start digging without fear of touching anything slimy.
c) tell her you'd really like to help but you have to go to the mall because you have a date with the fry guy to "figure out how the shake machine works."

5. Your mom suggests doing something constructive over summer break. You decide to:
a) volunteer at a hospital because you like helping people, and you'd like to

find out more about how things work there.

b) spend your time trying to figure out how to make the greatest chocolate chip, double fudge cookies in the universe.

c) see if you can find all of the constellations on your star map with the telescope you got for your birthday.

6. Your friend is working on a science project for school, but she's stumped and asks you to help. You:

a) tell her that you nearly blew up the lab during your chemistry experiment.

b) assure her that she came to the right person.

c) suggest that she watch the Discovery Channel instead.

7. The school science fair is coming and everyone must choose an area of science to explore. You:

a) almost faint and fall out of your seat because picking just one area to explore makes your head spin.

b) wonder if bringing in that moldy piece of cheese from the refrigerator at home counts as an experiment.

c) decide to choose an experiment by using the "eeny meany miny mo" method.

Scoring:

1. a.3 b.1 c.2
2. a.2 b.3 c.1
3. a.1 b.2 c.3
4. a.3 b.1 c.2
5. a.2 b.1 c.3
6. a.2 b.3 c.1
7. a.3 b.2 c.1

17–21 Points: You are definitely a scientist in the making! You want to figure out why things happen, what makes things work, and how things fit together. You already have a good foundation of scientific knowledge. Best of all—you're not afraid to use science in real life. Keep learning—science is like a good book: the deeper you go, the more you know!

12–16 Points: You have the kind of curiosity that's shared by all scientists. You're observant and like to try new things. Advice for you: spend some time reading about different scientific fields, focus on science, and then try to use your knowledge in your day-to-day life.

7–11 Points: Looks like science is still a secret to you! That's okay! It's never too early or too late to start thinking about how the world works and to begin asking questions. Did you know that asking questions is the basis of all science? It's true! Try asking some questions—and don't stop until you satisfy your curiosity. You'll be surprised at the interesting answers you will find.

Scientists do experiments, share what they learn, and learn from other people's mistakes as well as their own. Most use some variation of the "scientific method," the famous formula you've probably learned about in school.

The scientific method is just an outline—real scientists may use one part more than others. For example, wildlife biologists may spend a lot of time observing, and theoretical physicists do a lot more hypothesizing than testing. Most scientists also add steps that work for them, like "Take a break," or "Ask a friend." Science is problem-solving, and different people do it in different ways.

How to Create Your Own Experiment

If you want to design your own experiments, you can use the scientific method. This involves figuring out what you're trying to do, taking notes on what happens, and then using your notes and your brain to figure out what it all means. If you follow this method, you can do science anywhere. If you're careful, you'll be able to trust your results and recreate your experiments anytime.

The Scientific Method

Observation: Scientists are always watching the world. Watching, listening, and being aware of something (without trying to change it) is called "observing." Observe your surroundings. Write down the things you notice.

Are you curious about something you see, hear, taste, smell, or notice? Come up with a question about what you observe. This could be the basis for your experiment.

For example, imagine that you've planted three flowers in pots on your windowsill. You've noticed that all three flowers seem to be dying. You wonder, "Why are my flowers dying?"

Research: Has anyone else already figured out the answer to your question? You could check the library, ask around, or surf the Internet. In the case of your flowers, you might find some books about your specific type of flower that will tell you why they're not healthy.

Hypothesis: Using what you already know, you might have a good guess about the answer. Write down any interesting answers to your science question that you can think of—if you don't have any, start with silly ones and work up to serious ones. Since this is science, after all, try to figure out which answers make the most sense. Think about what you've seen and make an "educated guess"—a guess based on your own knowledge. This will be your hypothesis about what you have observed—what you think about what you see.

In your flower experiment, your hypothesis might be, "I think that my flowers are getting the wrong amount of water, and that's why they're dying." Now it's time to figure out if you're right.

Experiment: You'll never know if you're right unless you test your idea. There might be more than one way to test an idea, so it's a good idea to come up with a list of ways you might test your hypothesis.

One way to experiment with your flowers is to give each of the three flowers a different amount of water. You can give one flower more water than you used to. Another flower can receive less water. And the third flower can get the same amount of water as you were giving it before.

It's a really good idea to keep track of all the information you gather in one place—a notebook is great. Write down how much water you're giving each flower, and note which ones seem to be getting healthier.

Analyze Your Results: Did your experiment turn out the way you thought it would, or did it surprise you? If you measured something, compare your measurements. Also, notice where you are really sure about your data and where you are uncertain.

In the flower example, the results might be what you expected. Maybe the flower with the most water was the healthiest and your hypothesis was correct. Or maybe the experiment just gave you more questions. If all the flowers still died, you might wonder if they needed more sun or less sun. You can start the whole process over again (with some new flowers, of course!).

Conclusion: What do you think? Did the experiment support your idea, or make you doubt it? Do you know more than when you started?
Here's one possible conclusion to the flower experiment:

"The flowers need two cups of water every day in order to live and bloom on my windowsill."

You've learned something new about your flowers, but maybe you have further questions such as: "Do different kinds of flowers need different amounts of water?" or "Would my flowers grow better in larger flower pots?" If your flowers still died, that means your hypothesis was wrong. Does that mean your experiment didn't work? No! You found out something even more interesting than your original idea. You've realized that there is something else that is killing the flowers. You might have to do some serious research to figure this one out, get some friends involved, or even find an expert. By proving yourself wrong you could be on the road to finding out something even more important.

What If My Experiment Doesn't Work?

If your experiment surprises you, that's good. That's how you find out new things. A real experiment is an experience; it's exposing your ideas to the real world. There are three important steps to making every experiment a success, whether it "goes right" or not:

Take Notes, Lots of Notes: Notes provide clues to new ideas, help you keep track of your own work, and are great evidence to remind you (and your teachers!) how much work you've already done. Notes can also save you from having to redo something because you forgot how it worked the first time.

If something goes wrong, you can check your notes. You can also take notes on how it went wrong, to help you figure out what to do differently the next time.

Break It Down: Sometimes, a question, or an experiment, is just too big—for example, "How do plants grow?" It could take years to learn the answer from books, let alone discover it by experimenting. You might need to try a smaller part of your real question—like, "How much water do plants need?"

Don't Be Afraid: It's okay to "mess up" your experiment. Things break, things fall apart, things get lost. Plan ahead by using safety equipment and asking for help, so that you don't have to worry about getting hurt.

As long as you're safe, you can watch your accidents for new ideas. "Something burning on the stove" was the accidental beginning for at least two discoveries: cherries jubilee (yum!) and vulcanized rubber (not so yummy, but pretty useful).

How do you turn accidents into discoveries? Before you clean up your mess, take notes. Look for anything weird or surprising about your accident, and you might discover something. (At the very least, you can discover how to avoid the same accident next time.)

It's not a scientist's job to be right every time, or on the first try. We know we aren't perfect—our job is to learn from the world and to try to understand it better. Real science can be scary—not because it's physically dangerous (it usually isn't), but because you risk failure every time you try something new. Scientists learn new things every day, but they also fail. Good scientists may sometimes get discouraged, or take a break, but they keep trying different approaches until they get somewhere. When we finally arrive at an explanation that works, it's really amazing. It's an incredible feeling to know—not just accidentally guess right—but to know and have proof that you figured out how something works.

Ellen Henrietta Swallow Richards

1842–1911

"In an age when environment is changing, we must give knowledge greater distribution, even reorganization, to restore the human link to environment."

Ellen could hardly believe her eyes. In her hand she held a letter from the Massachusetts Institute of Technology—they had accepted her application! One of the best new science schools in the country was offering Ellen a chance no other woman had been given. Not only did they want her for a student, but they weren't going to charge her any money for tuition. She loved studying science, and knew that she would work hard at becoming a scientist. At that moment, Ellen Henrietta Swallow felt her dreams were about to come true.

Ellen Swallow was a poor farm girl who grew up in Dunstable, Massachusetts, in the 1850s. As a child, Ellen was always interested in exploring the world around the farm, and everything having to do with science. She wasn't afraid to get her hands dirty. Her dream was to go to a good school, maybe even to college, and then teach.

But Ellen didn't have the luxury of concentrating on schoolwork. Instead, she had to do all kinds of work to save money for private school: working on farms, teaching school, tutoring, cooking, cleaning, nursing, and helping in the family store. Her parents worked two jobs each, determined that she should have the best possible education. They even moved so that she could be near a better school.

After several years of working and learning bit by bit, Ellen was ready for college. She decided to go to the first women's college with science classes: Vassar. At Vassar, Ellen worked with the famous astronomer Maria Mitchell. Ellen loved school, and studied long hours. Ellen's hard work propelled her to graduation—she completed Vassar's program in only two years! But that wasn't enough school for a bright girl like Ellen.

Ellen wanted to continue studying science, and the best places to do that would only teach men. So she applied to MIT as a "special student." She was admitted free of charge. Ellen was delighted and grateful; this meant that she and her family wouldn't have to work so hard to pay for her school, and she could concentrate on her studies. It wasn't until later that Ellen found out the real reason she could attend the school for free. It wasn't just generosity: men sometimes got upset when the school started to teach women, so the school wanted an easy way out in case of trouble. If Ellen didn't pay tuition, officially she wasn't really a student! They could teach her, and give her a degree, without ever officially admitting her.

Ellen didn't worry too much about her position as the only young woman on campus—she was busy taking advantage of the opportunity to learn. She made sure that MIT wouldn't stop teaching her by doing important work—such as isolating a new chemical element, vanadium. In a few years she earned a Bachelor of Science degree and her teachers at Vassar decided to give her a Master of Arts degree for the same work!

After she graduated, Ellen continued to study chemistry at MIT, but the administration wouldn't let her earn a Ph.D. MIT officially voted not to admit women students, and it wasn't until about ten years later that they changed their minds. Ellen stayed around, though. She taught lab classes, and helped create a special lab for women until they were allowed to participate in regular classes. Two years after the first women students were "officially" admitted, MIT hired Ellen as a teacher.

Ellen developed whole new fields of science, like ecology, and sanitation engineering, nutrition, and home economics. And she was relentless in support of women's education. Ellen helped found the organization we now know as the American Association of University Women.

In 1875, Ellen and another MIT teacher, Robert Richards, fell in love and married. Their honeymoon was also a research trip to study mines and collect ore samples, with Robert's students along to help!

Ellen didn't believe that science belonged solely in the classroom—she thought that scientific methods could be applied to everyday life. For example, she realized that it was a bad idea to put the septic tank (toilet water) right next to a well for drinking water. The Richards immediately moved their septic tank to a more sensible location.

Maintaining a home is just as scientific as anything else, Ellen realized. Why not teach women scientific principles like hygiene, food chemistry, and financial math, so they could keep their families safe, healthy, and free from debt? Ellen organized a conference of people like herself who were interested in applying science to everyday human life, and they decided to call this new field of science "Home Economics," or "Domestic Science."

Now this may not seem like a big deal to us today, but in the 1800s women ran the home. At the time, most men were educated in their professions and trades, but there were few opportunities for women's education. Yet running a household requires the same skills as running a business—budgeting, buying supplies, and maintaining certain standards of health, cleanliness, and safety.

Ellen was a science pioneer in many ways. She was a skilled chemist, but what she did best involved finding new ways to make science useful for ordinary people. She developed ideas such as home economics and ecology as ways to make the world a little better, safer, and easier to live in.

Why Do You Love Science?

I believe that everyone can be a scientist, both women and men. A person who researches and invents things is a scientist. Scientists make the world a better place. It doesn't matter what religion you are, what race you are, or what age you are. If you're a woman or a man, you can do it! All you need is a dream, knowledge, hard work, and an analytical mind and you, too, can be a scientist.

—Erin Buerger, age 9

Science is my favorite subject in the world. There are all different kinds of science, but the three that stand out are: biology, chemistry, and physics. First, there is biology, the science of process and structure of living organisms. I like looking at slides and specimens. Next, there is chemistry, working with chemicals and seeing what happens when you mix them, as well as working with formulas. Last, but not least, is physics, which gives you an understanding of how things work. I enjoy putting things together as well as taking them apart and learning how things work. Science is one of the most important things in my life and I would not be able to fulfill my dream of becoming a veterinarian without it.

—Alicia Brodrick, age 13

Chapter 2

Dirt and Dinos: Earth Sciences

There's dirt on your jeans again from digging in the backyard. You found some ancient wood and a really cool crystal, and you would love to discover another arrowhead. Your bookcase is sagging under the weight of dozens of rocks, including translucent agates and three awesome fossils. On family road trips, you gaze at passing hills, rivers, and sand dunes, learning their patterns and looking for clues to the history of the land.

What inspires people to spend their lives digging in the dirt? Though some earth scientists do work in comfy places (like museums or corporate offices), many are happiest in harsh places where few people live, chipping away at rocks in the hot desert sun, or drilling into ancient glaciers. Why do they do it? Well, some gals just love adventure, and earth scientists often are required to go to remote places in the world to do their studies.

Some earth scientists—such as geologists, paleontologists, and archaeologists—don't just explore today's world, they "time-travel" through the earth to discover where dinosaurs hatched, when the first birds took flight, or how ancient warrior women rode to battle. Buildings, plants, and the traffic from modern life often cover up the deep layers that these scientists want to study. Sometimes you have to get away from it all to see anything. There's a lot of mystery and adventure in the earth sciences.

You might be thinking, "Adventures make good stories, but they don't sound too comfortable." Well, check out the earth science behind modern life. Did you ever wonder where the items you use each day come from? Resources to make colorful clothes, makeup, video games, movies, cars, roads, and buildings come from the Earth. Oil, coal, tar, rocks, and minerals are used to make everything from synthetic fabrics, plastics, and electronics to the chemicals in your sidewalks, snack foods, and camera film. By studying the mysteries of earth science, many mysteries of everyday life can be explained.

Early Fossil Hunters

Don't mind a little dirt under your nails? Neither did these women. One famous early fossil hunter, Mary Anning, was eleven years old in 1810 when she started selling fossils to support her family. Too poor to pay for an education, Mary taught herself by reading and exploring. She discovered England's first ichthyosaurus (which means "fish lizard" because they lived in the sea), and the world's first plesiosaur. Many male scientists at the time doubted Mary's abilities—they just couldn't figure out how an uneducated woman knew so much! But soon they were coming to Mary for advice on their own research. Luckily, today's earth scientists include a lot more women than they did in 1810, and women can now study at the best universities.

Careers in Earth Science

There are many different careers in the earth sciences. Scientists today work for private companies in industries such as oil, mining, construction, engineering, independent research, and environmental consulting. Governments hire earth scientists to work in agencies like the U.S. Environmental Protection Agency, Bureau of Land Management; military and civil engineering; and in state, county, and city departments like water, environment,

Quiz—Are the Earth Sciences for You?

1. When you think about dinosaurs and dirt, you feel an urge to:
a) watch *The Flintstones*.
b) dig in your backyard to see what you find.
c) go to the museum of natural history.

2. The thought of a T-rex:
a) is intriguing but makes your flesh crawl.
b) reminds you of the scene in *Jurassic Park* where a T-rex eats a lawyer, and you wonder if that could really happen.
c) sends you packing to the library to find out more.

3. You hear the word geology and you:
a) reach for a dictionary. What the heck is "geology" anyway?
b) pull out your rock collection and dust it off.
c) grab a shovel and start digging for samples in your backyard.

4. While walking in the woods, you:
a) spend all your time investigating the wonders of nature.
b) investigate the wonders of nature, but keep getting distracted by the thought of a bear attacking you.
c) think nature is fascinating, but that it has too many bugs that bite.

5. The weather woman says that there is a possibility of rain today, and you:
a) are thankful to have advanced knowledge, so you know to take your umbrella to school.
b) run outside to check your barometer.
c) wonder how she could possibly know, when she's always indoors.

6. For you, geography is about:
a) reading the map on family road trips.
b) studying the various physical, biological, and cultural features of the earth's surface.

c) trying to remember the capital of North Dakota.

7. While on an "Earth Science" field trip to the ocean, you:
a) study every little creature (plant or animal) you can find.
b) find the ocean vast and beautiful, but are preoccupied by the thought of getting seasick on the boat.
c) wonder what's the best way to cook the fish you just caught.

Scoring:
1. a.1 b.3 c.2
2. a.1 b.2 c.3
3. a.1 b.2 c.3
4. a.3 b.2 c.1
5. a.1 b.2 c.3
6. a.2 b.3 c.1
7. a.3 b.2 c.1

17–21 points: You have the right stuff to make a great geologist or paleontologist! You would love to go on a fossil dig, walk through an ancient cave, or study bizarre rock formations. You're not afraid to investigate the unknown. Keep going—these science dreams could be in your near future!

12–16 points: You may not know a whole lot about Earth Science, but you're on the right track. You appreciate the world around you, the beauty of the earth and its creatures, and would like to know more. Don't let your fears get in the way of exploring and trying new things.

7–11 points: Dirt? Bugs? Old bones? Gross! So, maybe the earth sciences aren't for you—you like modern conveniences and aren't afraid to show it. Still—try breaking out of your comfort zone. Put on a pair of old jeans and take a walk through a new landscape. Notice the shape and size of the mountains, hills, and valleys around you. You might even enjoy it!

sanitation, or transportation. Some scientists work for non-governmental organizations, such as the Nature Conservancy, the Audubon Society, the World Wildlife Fund, and many others.

Geologist: Geologists study the history of the earth by examining the layers of soil, rock, water, minerals, gases, molten magmas, and metals that make up the bulk of the planet. Geologists can specialize in different areas, such as minerals or meteorites. They work together to learn more about the earth's history and to find resources, enabling them to predict future geological events such as earthquakes, volcanic eruptions, and tidal flows.

Paleontologist: Most science fans know that paleontologists study fossils—remnants of ancient bones, leaves, or footprints. We can still find actual bones or bodies of creatures that lived tens of thousands of years ago, like saber-toothed tigers, cave bears, and ancient humans. Fossils give us clues about past life: early mammals, sea creatures, plants, and even tiny bacteria. By studying the past, paleontologists learn about how plants and animals have adapted to our ever-changing world.

Archaeologist: If you think rock art and ancient arrowheads are more interesting than dinosaur dung (or "coprolite" as it's called in the science world), you might be interested in the study of early humans. When we examine the actual *things* that early people left behind, that's archaeology. Archaeologists record everything from trash heaps and human remains and scraps, to treasure-filled tombs and ancient cities.

Anthropologist: These scientists study both ancient and modern cultures, learning how people feed themselves, live together, trade, fight, worship, and bury their dead. They also trace the relationships between different human races and cultures.

Geographers: Geographers make maps. They also study the relationships and distribution of the earth's resources, populations, industries, and governments. From schoolbooks to current affairs, geographers study how the earth relates to the people who live there.

Volcanologist: Ever been fascinated by red-hot magma bubbling out of a volcano? Then being a volcanologist might be for you. These daring scientists investigate the origin of volcanic rocks and the life cycles of volcanoes.

Oceanographers: Oceanographers investigate oceans, including marine organisms, water properties, and the history of the sea bottom. An oceanographer might dive undersea to protect endangered black coral, chart the currents using satellite data, or spend time on fishing boats and oil rigs showing people where to find undersea resources.

Meteorologist: Meteorologists study the weather, climate, and atmosphere. You probably know at least one meteorologist by name—your local TV weather forecaster. Other meteorologists might chart the jet stream, do research on ice and snow formations, track plumes of smog or dust, or develop computer models to predict future weather more accurately.

Geo-Jobs

When techniques from other sciences are used to study the earth, we can add "geo" to the name: geochemistry, geophysics, geo-biology, and hydro-geology.

Geophysicist: Geophysicists study the earth using techniques from physics: gravitational, magnetic, electrical, and seismic (earth-shaking) methods. They can tell you how big the Earth is, how heavy, what forces affect it, and how we can tell. Sometimes they study how the Earth compares to other planets.

Geobiologist: Did you know limestone is mostly made of microscopic seashells? Geobiologists study the effects living creatures have on non-living materials of the earth (like rocks and atmosphere), and how the earth's environments affect life. Geochemists study the chemical composition, properties, and relationships of the earth's materials.

Mary Nicol Leakey
1913–1996

"For me it was the sheer instinctive joy of collecting, or indeed one could say treasure hunting: it seemed that this whole area abounded in objects of beauty and great intrinsic interest that could be taken from the ground."

"Fire!"

Girls shrieked and everyone ran to the classroom door, away from the cause of the loud noise. The nuns who ran the convent school ushered the students through the smoke to the exit, fearing a catastrophic explosion. In the back of the classroom, sitting next to her destroyed chemistry experiment, thirteen-year-old Mary Nicol tried to smother her giggles.

She wasn't laughing later when her mother found out that she had deliberately caused the explosion. This was the second time Mary had been expelled from school.

Mary didn't try to cause trouble. She actually liked learning, but hated school and didn't have many friends. Lonely, and still grieving over the death of her father, Mary's impulsive ideas sometimes led her to trouble. Mary's father, Erskine Nicol, was a painter who had a special interest in Egyptology and prehistoric art. He had taken his only daughter on walks to look for interesting stones, and to see the ancient drawings in the caves near their home in France. The Nicol family traveled often in Italy, France, Switzerland, and England. Mary never attended formal school until she was thirteen, after her father died. Mary's mother moved the family back to England, where Mary was sent to a convent to study.

Despite Mary's rough times at school, she remained interested in prehistoric art, and was fascinated when her mother took her on a trip to Stonehenge. Like her father, she was an excellent artist, and it was her drawings that eventually led to her well-known career in archaeology.

When Mary was a teenager, she met the famous archaeologist Dorothy

Liddell, who asked Mary to be her assistant at a Stone Age archaeological site in England. Mary was thrilled! At the site, Mary drew pictures of the stone tools that the archaeologists discovered. Eventually, her pictures were published. Mary was excited that she could combine both her passions—art and archaeology—into a rewarding learning experience.

In 1933, at the age of 20, Mary attended a lecture given by Louis Leakey, a well-known archaeologist who had just returned from a trip to Africa. Louis was so impressed with Mary's drawings that he asked her to illustrate his upcoming book, *Adam's Ancestors*. It was the beginning of a long relationship that would put their names down in the history books. Mary and Louis married three years later, on Christmas Eve.

Mary and Louis Leakey spent most of their time researching in Africa, often taking their three sons and several Dalmatians on their expeditions. They didn't just study the ruins of famous cultures like Egypt. The Leakeys wanted to know about the earliest origins of humankind—they worked in a branch of archaeology called "paleoanthropology." The Leakeys studied human culture and evolution by looking at the fossils of early humans, or hominids. They worked together to answer the questions, "Where did humans come from?" and "When did humans first exist?" Not many scientists thought to look in Africa for the answers, but Louis and Mary were convinced that was where they would find important clues in the mystery of human evolution.

One of the most important discoveries of Mary's career came one July morning in 1959, when Louis was home in bed, sick with the flu. She went to work without him, taking two dogs, Sally and Victoria. In the gorge where they had been digging, she noticed a piece of bone sticking out of the ground. Stooping down to uncover more bone, she realized that this was not just any bone, but a whole skull. Mary hurried back to camp to tell Louis what she had found. This was the man they were searching for—the missing link in human evolution! Dragging himself out of bed, Louis examined the skull with Mary, and together they excavated the entire skull, which had belonged to a man who lived 1.75 million years ago—later deemed "the world's earliest man." They named him Zinjanthropus, meaning "man from East Africa."

Mary and Louis went on to make many more discoveries in Africa. After the discovery of Zinjanthropus, they decided to excavate the entire site where the bones had been found. This was a huge task, and Louis couldn't get away from his museum curator's job very often. Mary took over the project, which took almost a year. She not only hired a crew and directed the dig, but got down in the trenches with the workers, digging and swinging a heavy pick. Mary's thoroughness and detailed recordings were praised by many fellow archaeologists. Hard work paid off for Mary and her crew: they found thousands of fossils, large implements, and bone fragments.

When Louis died, Mary continued to work, often with her son Richard, who had inherited his parents' love of archaeology. "Leakey's luck," as many in the field called it, was still with them, and throughout the years many more important discoveries were made.

Mary died in 1996, but the Leakey legend lives on. Her daughter-in-law Maeve and granddaughter Louise Leakey carry on the Leakey tradition, exploring Africa, making new discoveries, and teaching people more about paleoanthropology and the beginnings of humankind.

What It Takes to Be an Earth Scientist

How do you become an earth scientist? If you think that rocks are interesting, you don't mind getting dirty, and you are persistent, you're well on your way. Learn all that you can; don't hesitate to try science camps that can teach you about the earth sciences, or to talk your folks into a summer field trip to see people working in the earth sciences. Study geology and biology in school and at the library, collect (legally!) what interests you, and start applying for summer jobs working on archeological digs or geological surveys when you're in high school.

Most professional earth scientists have at least some college education, and many have an advanced degree (like a Ph.D.) in their fields. Anyone can be an amateur rockhound or fossil-hunter without a fancy degree, though—all it takes is patience, interest, and the perseverance to get your collections home. (Did we mention that rocks are heavy?)

Earthy Experiments

Dig into these ideas if you want to get the real scoop on earth science.

Scratch Test: Found any good rocks lately? What's your hardest rock? Take a couple of different rocks, and scratch one against the other. The softer rock should leave a streak, like pencil or chalk, on the harder one; the harder rock should scratch the softer one. If neither of these things happens, the two rocks may have about the same hardness. (Just scratch gently—don't try to break rocks by hand.)

You can use this test to "rate" your rocks: Is each rock harder than your fingernail? Harder than your sidewalk? Softer rocks might be good as drawing "chalk"; medium ones can be carved into sculptures. The hardest rocks make durable buildings, jewelry, and tools.

Muddy Waters: Grab a clear jar with a lid. Then go outside and scoop up some earth—dirt, pebbles, mud, sand, wet muck. Add water to fill the jar. (It's easiest to do this experiment near a river or pond.)

Place the lid securely on the jar and shake it all up. Then watch everything settle back down. What settles first? How long does it take? Do you see any layers or colors? Draw or write down whatever you see.

Let the jar sit still for a while. Examine the materials with a magnifying glass, or "excavate" each layer with a spoon. What else do you notice? You can compare different kinds of dirt this way. Compare garden and potting soils, riverside mud, and dry roadside dust. What can you discover about plain old dirt?

Why Do You Love Science?

Out of all the many, many little subjects that fit under the category of science, I'm really interested in archaeology. I love finding out about ancient times and our ancestors' daily lives. I also like experimenting. In my case, it's usually trying to duplicate Greek art or Roman buildings. I think that archaeology is like a time machine, giving you knowledge about your past and painting a picture of how easy or how hard the past was. I personally think that even though the past may have been difficult to live in, it still interests me. In fact, it makes me want to try even harder to fulfill my dream of becoming an archaeologist.

—Hannah Bartlett, age 12

When I grow up, one of the things I would like to be is a geologist. Geologists study different things about the earth, like rocks, soil, and insects. A year ago I began to be interested in studying earthworms. In my state it rains a lot, and when it rains hundreds of earthworms crawl out of the earth and onto sidewalks and the blacktop. Many of my girlfriends thought worms were gross and disgusting! I thought that earthworms were fascinating. I began to read books about them and went online to get information. I formed a club at school for girls who were interested in studying earthworms. At every recess on rainy days we collected earthworms and we started a worm farm. I think girls are told that they shouldn't like certain things like bugs or earthworms. But you have to be strong and brave to stick to what you like, no matter what people say.

—Amanda Jones, age 8

Science is one of my favorite subjects in school, because as we study, we realize that science is all around us! We recently studied about land forms, or earth science. Our class did lots of experiments using sand, water, and other objects. Our teacher gave us miniature houses, people, and animals. We were told to figure out a way to build a town that would be safe from flooding or wind or other natural weather elements. We saved our town by making a ditch for the water and placing the town high enough up on a sand mountain we had built, and secure enough into the ground, that no damage was done by water or wind! Our teacher was so proud of us! I enjoy learning about science . . . and hope that other kids enjoy it—finding science all around them and experiencing the fun of learning, just like me.

—Janelle Britton, age 11

Chapter 3

Lions and Tigers and Bears, Oh MY! Animal Biology

Your house resembles a zoo, complete with an aquarium full of fish and various caged rodents. You love making sure they all have comfortable, clean homes, and good food to eat. Now you're trying to figure out how to convince your parents they should let you keep yet another stray cat . . .

It doesn't matter if you live in an apartment in the big city, or out on the farm—there are interesting, living things everywhere. Every day you interact with plants, animals, humans, and germs. It can be easy not to focus on the living, thriving world around you, but if you tend to notice weird beetles or a cool bird flying by, if you care about animals, or if you want to help cure the world's worst diseases, you might have the makings of a biologist.

Biologists study everything that's alive, including bacteria, plants, animals, fungi, and protozoans (microscopic, one-celled animals). For this chapter, we will focus mainly on animal biology.

As an animal biologist, you might swim with dolphins to learn more about them, or research cures for diseases in a laboratory. You might design new homes for animals at zoos, or engineer prosthetic limbs for people who have been injured. Biologists study everything from the virus that causes the flu to the traveling patterns of gray whales. Ultimately, biology is the science of life!

Bio Girls

There have been tons of extraordinary women who have contributed to the field of biology. In 1946, Elizabeth Hazen and Rachel Brown invented the first fungicide that could protect people from fungus infections. Patricia Bath invented laser eye surgery to help people see better. Another field where biology makes a huge difference is in developing new medicines. Gertrude Bell Elion, a medical researcher, has obtained at least forty-five different medical patents, including treatments for leukemia, gout, and organ transplantation.

Biology Careers

Biology can be used in many different careers. You can use your biology knowledge to go to medical school or veterinary school. You may decide you like working in a lab, researching cures for diseases, or you may prefer to do field research, observing animals in the wild. If you think you might be interested in biology, you should learn more about these careers:

Zoologist: One day you're working with the Australian wallaby and the next you're feeding grass to an elephant. A zoologist works with many different animals and they don't necessarily work in a zoo. Many zoologists get to work out in the field, observing animals in their natural habitats. They learn about the histories of the different kinds of animals, how they relate to their environments, and how they "talk" and interact with each other.

Some other animal-related sciences:

Ichthyologist: An ichthyologist studies fish. They observe fish in the wild, and in the laboratory. They may be finding ways to conserve wild fish populations, helping keep zoo and pet fish healthy, or managing fish farms or fisheries.

Quiz—Is Biology in Your Future?

1. Your friends say, "When it comes to animals,
a) you've got the magic touch, animals respond well to you."
b) you've got the tragic touch, you should look, not touch."
c) getting that goldfish was ideal for you."

2. The outdoors makes you:
a) break out in hives!
b) run upstairs to pack a bag chock full of goodies, like a magnifying glass, tweezers, and specimen jars.
c) want to go for a hike and observe the interesting animals and plants you might come across.

3. When your little brother gets sick, you:
a) call grandma to come over and show you how to make her famous get better-quicker-chicken soup.
b) regard him with sympathy . . . from a distance.
c) take notes on his symptoms and consult a reference manual.

4. People are always telling you that you are:
a) calm under pressure.
b) thoughtful and patient.
c) too nervous even to cut your own toenails.

5. Your biology teacher gives you the task of dissecting an insect. You:
a) do all you can to repress your gag reflex.
b) think it's kind of sad, but are excited to gain some insight.
c) just want to skip that class and come back the next day for the results.

6. The idea of memorizing the animal classification system makes you:
a) get a throbbing headache!
b) take out your pad and pen because you're going to take notes, which will come in handy for your next trip to the zoo.
c) wonder if snails are really related to your brother.

7. When it comes to taking care of animals, you:
a) make Dr. Dolittle envious.
b) like to take care of them, even if it takes time away from other activities that you like.
c) have trouble keeping even a goldfish alive.

Scoring:
1. a.3 b.1 c.2
2. a.2 b.3 c.1
3. a.2 b.1 c.3
4. a.3 b.2 c.1
5. a.1 b.3 c.2
6. a.1 b.3 c.2
7. a.3 b.2 c.1

17–21 points: If you dream of becoming a veterinarian or medical doctor, then you are on the right track! You are curious about the living body, how it works, and how to fix it when something goes wrong. You love animal biology and experimentation. Maybe someday, when someone shouts, "Is there a doctor in the house?" you can reply, "That's me!"

12–16 points: You like animals, but they are not really your passion. You're interested in medicine and microbiology, though, and different treatments to make people feel better. You would make a great lab technician or microbiologist.

7–11 points: Well, you probably don't dream of becoming a veterinarian, which is a big relief to all the animals out there! If you'd like to know more about animals, get some books and read all you can about them. Start small—try owning a goldfish or rat, even an ant farm. You don't have to hold them to realize how amazing they are.

Ornithologist: Ornithology is the study of birds. An ornithologist may study rare, endangered birds and their habitats or work in a museum, educating people about the many different kinds of birds in the world.

Herpetologist: A herpetologist studies reptiles and amphibians. As a herpetologist, you can spend time in the wild, studying animals like turtles, snakes, lizards, frogs, or alligators, and observing their behavior. Or you may prefer to work at a university or museum, where you can work in a laboratory doing research. You may even be studying new species!

Veterinarian: If you're a Dr. Dolittle at heart and would like to fix the aches and pains of Fido and Fluffy, then being a veterinarian might be for you. Vets specialize in the healing and prevention of disease in animals, both pets and farm animals.

Wildlife Manager: Hanging out with the birds and the bees in the great outdoors—what could be better? Wildlife managers get to do research on and help protect animals and endangered species.

Physician: You might be helping a tennis star get her swing back, or performing a heart transplant on an infant. Doctors make a huge impact on everyone's lives. There are doctors who specialize in just about everything, from your ears to your toes.

Microbiologist: Microbiologists study bacteria, viruses, fungus, and single-celled organisms. We need mini organisms to digest our food, produce the oxygen that we breathe, and get rid of wastes. Microbiologists make discoveries that often improve lives and make the world a better place. Just think: without some of their amazing scientific finds, lots of medicines wouldn't be available to help people get well.

Getting Started in Biology

Biology takes a lot of curiosity and patience. If you are interested in working as a biologist, you will need to take biology classes (of course!) and also

Dian Fossey
1932–1985

"There was no way that I could explain . . . my compelling need to return to Africa to launch my long-term study of the gorillas. Some may call it destiny and others may call it dismaying. I call the sudden turn of events in my life fortuitous."

Dian was inconsolable. Her beloved goldfish Goldie was floating belly-up in her fishtank. It was the only pet Dian was allowed to have. Her mother and stepfather would not allow other, "dirty" animals in the house.

"I cried for a week when I found him . . . . My parents thought it was good riddance, so I never got another," wrote Dian many years later. Though young Dian didn't get another pet, her passion for animals never faded. She had dreams of seeing the world, and the exotic animals that lived in distant lands.

Dian Fossey grew up in Northern California with her mother and stepfather. Her parents were strict, but Dian did her best to follow the rules. In college she attempted to study business because her parents wanted her to. She hated it. She worked on all of her vacations to save money for school, sometimes working at a factory, or a department store. Finally, she enrolled in a veterinary medicine course at a new school. Dian loved working with animals. Unfortunately, she failed chemistry and physics—two sciences required to become a veterinarian. She eventually got her degree in occupational therapy instead, but she never lost her desire to work with animals.

After school, Dian worked for several years with children who had physical and emotional disabilities. She liked working with the kids, but still dreamed of adventure. When she heard that her best friend was planning an expedition to Africa, Dian started saving every penny and taking out loans so that she could also go to Kenya and Tanzania, in East Africa.

When Dian finally obtained the money for the trip, she was ecstatic. She read everything she could about Africa, and was particularly intrigued by a book called *The Year of the Gorilla* by zoologist George Schaller. Dian was thrilled to finally have the chance to see African wildlife.

She took pictures constantly, and wrote in her journal about all the species she was seeing. "Bristly warthogs and baboons everywhere. Buffalo, then rhino . . . Sykes monkey, Colobus monkey, crested cranes . . . " she noted. "Saw five male lions, herds of wildebeest, zebra, impala . . . " But what she really wanted to see were gorillas.

Most people at this time feared gorillas, which conjured up images of King Kong-type monsters. They were thought to be cruel creatures that liked to attack humans. Still, Dian wanted to observe these creatures in their habitat, to see what they were really like. She set out to find a guide who would take her to them. One day six gorillas warily approached her group, and Dian was fascinated. They did not seem monstrous to her. After her first gorilla sighting on this trip, Dian knew she would come back someday to study these magnificent animals.

Dian returned to Africa in 1966. She had the support of Louis Leakey, a world-famous archaeologist also working in Africa (see the biography of his wife, Mary Nicol Leakey on page 26). Dian spent her first few days with Jane Goodall, well-known for her research with chimpanzees. In 1967, Dian began observing gorillas in Zaire. Soon she moved to Rwanda, where she started the Karisoke Research Center. Because she had failed science in school, she had no formal training as a scientific researcher. Dian had to learn as she went along.

Dian lived in a cabin, which became her home for the next eighteen years. She spent much of her time observing the gorillas in their natural habitat. She watched them, and in time learned to imitate their sounds and habits. She did this to get closer to the gorillas, without them charging her or running away.

Her research was important because no researcher had yet been able to get as close to gorillas in the wild as Dian did. She learned about their behavior and wrote down everything she observed. Her research revealed to people that gorillas were not monsters. She sat within a few feet of them to observe, and was not harmed. She even had contact with some of them, and made friends with a gorilla she called Digit.

Poaching was an ever-growing problem in the region where Dian worked, even though it was a protected national park. Gorillas were killed by traps meant for antelope. Poachers also made money from selling dead gorillas as "trophies." Gorillas were in danger of becoming extinct. When Dian's friend Digit was killed by poachers, Dian launched a campaign to stop the slaying.

Dian eventually went back to school to get her Ph.D. in zoology from Cambridge University, in England. She wrote a book about her work with the gorillas in Africa, called *Gorillas in the Mist* (later made into a movie by the same name). She missed Africa, though, and in 1983 returned to be with her gorillas once more.

On December 26, 1985, Dian Fossey was found murdered in her cabin; many believed she had been killed by poachers for revenge. The mystery of her tragic death was never solved. Her love for the gorillas and her unique research are still famous among biologists. Dian was buried in the graveyard she had created for the gorillas. Her gravestone reads: "No one loved gorillas more . . . "

chemistry, math, physics, and computer classes for organizing your data. English and writing classes are also important, because biologists spend a lot of time writing down their theories and observations. Many biology careers require a four-year college degree. You can get extra experience by volunteering at a veterinarian's office, zoo, animal shelter, or hospital.

Biological Observations

Biologists sometimes observe, and sometimes experiment. You can try both:

Bird Biology: Try watching birds. Notice the sounds they make, and the ways they move. Are the birds eating, carrying stuff, or interacting with each other? What might they be "talking" about? (Do they sound different when there's a cat nearby?)

Grab a notepad and sketch some of the birds. Try to show different features that you notice, like beak shape, tail feathers, or different colors. (You don't have to make a pretty drawing, just one that helps you remember what you saw.)

When you're done, write a paragraph about the birds' behavior. Can you think of ways to attract more birds to your yard, based on your observations? Bird-watching builds wildlife biology skills; it's also a popular hobby around the world.

Microbiology: Put an orange peel in a glass jar outside, and another one in your basement or garage. Leave the jars there for 2–4 days. What happens to the orange peel? Are there any differences between the two jars? Examine the peels with a magnifying glass. Did you know that penicillin, the world's first antibiotic (medicine that kills germs already inside people), is related to orange peel mold?

You can try this with other things—lettuce, fruits, vegetable scraps. What grows on each one? (Meat, eggs, and cheese are not a great idea: they stink, attract pests, and become poisonous.) Be sure to label your experiments so they don't get thrown out, and clean up when you're done—especially remember to wash your hands.

Why Do You Love Science?

Ever since the moment my seventh grade biology class stepped into our classroom to find trays of gelatinous cow eyeballs on our lab tables, my career field was set. As my friends moaned and twisted their mouths with loud exclamations of "Dis-gust-ing!" I literally widened my eyes so not to miss any part of the dissection demonstration. In elementary school, I had made up my mind to become a "kids' doctor"—a pediatrician—but it was only in seventh grade that I truly comprehended the many different career opportunities that deal with science. After all, in what other subject besides science did we get to play in dirt? I plan to study hard now, and continue to learn more, far into the future, as there is always something new to learn, something new to discover. —Victoria Shum, age 17

I love so many things about science! Science makes life a whole, big adventure full of learning and innovation. Science makes people's lives easier, yet more suspenseful. Nobody knows what's going to be unearthed next. Without science, where would we be? No wheel, no sanitation, no electricity, no chance of medical operations or fighting disease, no resource conservation. Right now I'm doing the Nature Trail Volunteer Program with the San Francisco Zoo. Teaching young children about working with animals

makes me so much more patient, understanding, welcoming, optimistic, and downright amazed. If the children I'm teaching enjoy the creatures, they may someday become zoologists and the next generation of scientists to explore the conservation and education of people and animals around the globe.

—Elizabeth Rosen, age 11

I love science and pigeons. I have about eighteen homing pigeons. They are really unique birds. They can fly back to their home from very far away. My family has taken my pigeons to Washington D.C., Niagara Falls, and Canada. They always fly back home. They can fly without stopping for about 500 miles. The biggest mystery for me is how my pigeons find their way home. I would love to study them  *and solve this mystery! Many scientists around the world think that this mystery is important, too. At Cornell University, and other universities in Europe, scientists study pigeons. When I get older I am going to design some interesting experiments to learn even more about them. Really, I enjoy all kinds of science, but pigeons are my favorite.*

—Catherine Mézes, age 9

Chapter 4

Technology: Computer Science and Mathematics

Your little brother has once again jammed the printer. Your grandma asks you to explain just how this e-mail thing works. The computer screen is flashing an angry error message, but are you worried? No way. It seems like someone is always asking you for help when it comes to the computer. You pull the jammed paper out of the printer, give your grandma a quick lesson about the Internet, and make the computer happy again. You sit back, relax, and pop in your favorite CD-ROM game . . .

Last time you were browsing your favorite Web site, did you think about how the information got on your screen? Every day, you are using technology that wouldn't exist without computer science and the mathematics behind it.

So does this mean that chatting with your friends over instant messenger or playing video games instead of doing your science homework counts as "studying?" Well, probably not . . . but it means that you might really enjoy some of the things that computer scientists do every day. They love computers, solving puzzles, using math, and thinking up new and creative solutions to problems. If you already spend lots of time at your computer and like cutting-edge stuff (like robot pets or virtual reality games), computer science or mathematics could be for you.

Math and Computer Savvy Women

One of the most famous early mathematics clubs was the school of Pythagoras. These philosopher-mathematicians believed that numbers were not only useful—they were keys to the secrets of nature and human life. Unlike many of the early Greek schools, the school of Pythagoras welcomed intelligent women and girls, including Pythagoras's wife, Theano, and their two daughters. Theano and her daughters assigned mystical meanings to the relationships between numbers, and supported their theories with logical and systematic reasoning. With attention to logical detail, the Pythagorean family's work provided important foundations for modern mathematics and science.

Many successful computer programmers team up with friends, co-workers, and assistants to help produce, test, and share ideas. Rear Admiral Grace Hopper and Howard Aiken led one famous team at Harvard, starting in 1944. They kept reinventing computers, making them into sophisticated devices that could be programmed using a special language and codes. Computer programmer Roberta Williams created the world's first graphic-based computer game in 1979.

Careers in Mathematics and Computer Science

Computer science involves the study of computers, from hardware (circuits, drives, memory, processors) to software (operating systems, and useful programs like Word, Internet browsers, and games). Mathematics is the science of numbers and their operations in different equations. There are lots of jobs that use math and computer science. Here are a few of them:

Computer Programmer: Computer programmers do everything from creating new software programs to cracking top-secret codes for the government. They use computer languages like UNIX, HTML, and Javascript to instruct computers.

Quiz—Are Computers for You?

1. If math were a sport, you would:

a) win first place.

b) be a contender.

c) contribute . . . as a spectator.

2. Your grandfather needs some help setting up his new PC. You:

a) know just who to recommend that he call.

b) pull up a chair and dive in.

c) tell him he can do it, and walk him through the steps.

3. You think computer games:

a) are a blast—you know all the cheat codes, and they give you ideas for your own game.

b) are fun if you know all the cheat codes.

c) are something you just can't seem to master.

4. You think geometry would be great for:

a) figuring out how to rearrange your room.

b) picking the best snowboard run on the mountain.

c) joining the same study group your crush attends.

5. One day when you're bored, your dad suggests you create your own Web site. You:

a) ask him if he can show you how to get started.

b) look at him and say, "Have you forgotten about the time I wiped out the entire hard drive?"

c) say, "Of course, why didn't I think of that," and get to work on the HTML code.

6. Your favorite programming language:

a) doesn't yet exist—you're working on it.

b) is any of them found in a programming manual.

c) "What's a programming language?"

7. When it comes to computers, you:
a) could spend all day on one.
b) enjoy spending a few hours here and there.
c) use it to check your email and get the latest news.

Scoring:
1. a.3 b.2 c.1
2. a.1 b.2 c.3
3. a.3 b.2 c.1
4. a.2 b.3 c.1
5. a.2 b.1 c.3
6. a.3 b.2 c.1
7. a.3 b.2 c.1

17–21 points: Get out the pocket PC! You're a real whiz—you can do things with a computer that most of your friends find impossible. You even enjoy math! Congratulations on your skills—now take them to the next level. Watch out, Bill Gates!

12–16 points: Although you like computers and can play on one for hours, you don't know a lot about the computer code or mathematics that makes software work. Challenge yourself once in a while by using the "Help" function on the computer to solve a problem, or using a little math when you budget your next allowance.

7–11 points: No, a hard drive is not a trip to your grandma's! You don't know a whole lot about computers, but you like to use them for games and writing papers. You may not be interested in math, either, but that's okay. You probably don't see a computer as a "science" but more as a machine to make your life easier.

Animator: Computer animators use specialized graphics software to create sophisticated visual effects for movies and TV.

Video Game Designer: This could be more fun than actually playing video games (and, hopefully, you'd get paid for it)! Video game designers create the characters, the settings, and even the story or "plot" of the game (if there is one). They may also work on the programming, to make sure each video game is challenging and fun.

Cryptologist: Cryptologists encipher or decipher messages into secret, often numeric, codes. Finding problems that are easy to write but very hard to solve is a good basis for a numerical code—if you can make a problem very difficult for even the most brilliant mathematician and fastest computer to solve, you can use it to make a code that will be very hard to crack.

Information Systems Specialist: Technology experts help people and companies to use their computers and protect themselves from problems. Mathematicians working in information systems develop ways to turn numbers into graphs, maps, and charts to answer complicated questions. Business people, scientists, and governments look to information specialists for help in tracking and interpreting their data.

Math Educator: Teaching and sharing the cool parts of math can take place in universities, colleges, high schools, elementary schools, or public science programs. Writing mathematical instruction books and talking to friends and kids about math and computer science are other great ways to spread information.

Statistician: These scientists deal a lot with numbers and study how often certain events occur. This lets us know how meaningful science results are, and how likely certain events are, and helps determine fair rates for insurance policies and pensions.

Economics, Finance, and Accounting Systems Specialist: Money flows around the world, and someone has to keep track of it. Economists, finan-

Ada Byron King

1815–1852

"Ada Byron, Lady Lovelace, was one of the most picturesque characters in computer history."
—**Betty Toole**, author of *Ada: The Enchantress of Numbers*

"How does this machine work?" seventeen-year-old Ada Byron asked. She was at one of her first parties in London society, and was talking to Charles Babbage, one of the most important scientists in the 1800s. Mr. Babbage's "Difference Engine" was the talk of the party, and Ada was excited by the idea of a machine that could calculate all on its own. Delighted by young Ada's interest in his invention, Mr. Babbage invited her and her mother to his house to see the machine.

Babbage's living room was crowded with people when Ada arrived. Many others were there to gawk at the contraption, wondering whether it could have any practical use. Ada, a pale, dark-haired girl whom her mother called "the bird," was usually quiet and withdrawn in groups of people—but not today. She walked right up to the machine to see it work. It counted, calculated sums, and did complicated equations—all tasks that were usually performed by people. Ada understood at once what a great invention this was, and saw its potential.

This first glimpse of the Difference Engine was an important moment in Ada Byron's life. She was fascinated by this "thinking machine," or computer, and eventually wrote the first computer programming language.

Ada Byron began her studies at the young age of five, in a time when it was believed that women could never be as good as men at something like mathematics. Ada's mother, Lady Byron, took a passionate interest in Ada's education. She hired tutors for her daughter, and when they weren't good enough, Lady Byron took over teaching Ada herself. She made sure that Ada's lessons included a great deal of science and math and other logical subjects. Lady Byron wanted to make sure Ada was well-grounded in science so that she wouldn't turn out like her father, the famous poet Lord Byron.

Ada didn't remember her father; her parents were officially separated before Ada was even six months old. Rumors of Lord Byron's scandalous behavior were circulating in society—his various love affairs, drinking habits, and large debts were well known. Many people of the time found his writing too outrageous. Lord and Lady Byron parted on such bad terms that all portraits of him were covered up so that Ada would not see him. After the separation, Lord Byron left England in disgrace, never to see Ada again. Though she never knew him, Ada's father was like a shadow in Ada's life.

When Ada was eight years old her father died, and was refused burial in the cemetery where all the other nobles in England were buried. Ada's mother had no desire to see Ada grow up to be a romantic poet like her father, and so she worked her daughter hard, often making her study from early morning until late in the evening. Ada was taught math, science, and foreign languages. If she acted naughty or didn't study hard enough, she was shut in her room alone as punishment. While Ada studied hard, sometimes the pressure would get to her and she would feel ill from "too much mathematics." Still, Ada wanted to please her mother, and proved to be an excellent student.

After seeing Mr. Babbage's Difference Engine as a teenager, Ada's world changed. Up until that point she had only learned elementary mathematics. Now she yearned for more. She wrote to one of her old tutors, begging to be taught more advanced mathematics like algebra and calculus. Ada also kept up her correspondence with Mr. Babbage.

As Ada grew up, she had many different tutors and had an intellect to make her mother proud. She corresponded with professors and learned more about math and science through this correspondence. Her pen-pal tutors would often send her problems to work out, and she would write them back with the answers and more questions.

In 1842, an Italian engineer named Menabrea wrote a paper about Babbage's Analytical Engine (the next invention Babbage planned to make). Ada translated Menabrea's article into English and, at Mr. Babbage's urging, decided to add her own "Notes" as well.

Ada's "Notes" were three times as long as Menabrea's original article, and even corrected Menabrea's errors. Ada also included some "programs"—instructions to make the engine do what the operator asked. (Program a machine? But this was a hundred years before the personal computer was even invented!) Her translation and notes were published in a scientific journal, which won her praise from many people. Charles Babbage said that he thought Ada understood his machine better than he did!

It wasn't until a century after Ada died that the first practical computers were actually built and put to work. In 1980, the U.S. military announced that they had decided on a standard programming language for all of their computer systems. This language was called Ada.

cial experts, and accountants figure out the rules for how it flows and how to make it grow. They manage money for individuals, corporations, and governments.

Computer Technician: These experts use their skills with mathematics and electronics to keep computers working in new ways, develop new computer capabilities, and keep computers up and running.

Mathematician: Some people like math so much, they need experiments to go with it. These people are mathematicians and spend time figuring out and developing new mathematical relationships and equations.

What it Takes to Do Computer Science or Math

Women of all ages are computer scientists and mathematicians. In school they studied problem solving, algebra, calculus, physics, chemistry, and programming. Most computer scientists also study math, because many of the equations and relationships common to mathematics are also used in computer programming.

Practical Math Projects

There are lots of games and crafts (like origami) that use math for fun, and at school you get math homework. But do you ever just use math around the house?

Scale Space: Do you ever think about rearranging your room? Create a scale model of your room, with each piece of furniture, and a tiny version of yourself. (You can do this with computer software, on graph paper, or in 3-D in a cardboard box.) Measure each thing, and then draw a miniature version using your measurements: one foot in real life could be one inch in your model, for example.

Try moving furniture around in the model to find the best fit. If you really want to redo your room, you can use your model to estimate the cost involved. Based on your model, can you figure out the amount of paint, curtains, shelves, or other materials you would need?

Budget Blues: Where does all your money go? Make a graph to show how much money you spend on clothes, food and snacks, and entertainment. What would you say you spend, on average, in a week? Try keeping track for a couple of weeks or months. (You can calculate averages by dividing the total amount of money you've spent by the number of weeks or days involved.)

Do you feel you're spending money wisely? You could use the graph to discuss a raise in your allowance—how can your parents say no to science?

Why Do You Love Science?

Science is one thing that I love. I like to think about how everything relates to science. For example, I really like to crew and kayak. My mother taught my brothers and my brothers taught me that rowing is a pattern of motion, like the special rowing motion called the "sweep." If you row on a crew team, you have to synchronize every stroke. The timing in rowing is mathematical. Also, science happens when you row. One oar goes under the water and you don't have much stability with the water that's pushing against it, so you need an opposite force to pull it up. This moves the boat but it also adds to the pressure on the oar so you might tip the boat—you always try not to "catch a crab" (tip over). I've caught a lot of crabs! I like to experience all kinds of science. I like to do new things and figure out what they are all about. **—Elizabeth Bagdorf, age 9**

Chapter 5

Mother Nature: Plant Biology, Ecology, and the Environment

It's your favorite time of year to hike—spring is in full bloom and flowers and leaves are busting out everywhere. You love learning the names of plants and animals. After an afternoon hike, you find your pockets are full of strange-shaped leaves, wild fruits, moss, rocks, and feathers. Every book in your room is already filled with pressed plants, and you can't wait to plant your own vegetable garden!

No creature lives alone—each living thing depends on a community of other plants, animals, insects, and the networks they create. This community of life is called an ecosystem ("eco" comes from the Greek word *oikos* meaning "home"), and each creature's immediate surroundings are called its environment. Environmental scientists study ecosystems all over the world, and how they affect and can improve our quality of life.

Quiz—Is Environmental Science for You?

1. For you, recycling is:
a) a must, you wouldn't think of doing otherwise.
b) something you do when there is a recycling receptacle available.
c) riding your bike more than once a day because it's good exercise.

2. The movie *Twister* inspired you to spend time:
a) building a tornado shelter.
b) studying weather patterns.
c) watching the Weather Channel.

3. If you had a choice, you would live:
a) in the city.
b) in the suburbs.
c) in the country.

4. When it comes to crawly things, you:
a) know the difference between a worm and a weevil.
b) find them interesting—from a distance.
c) prefer to read about worms and weevils in the relative safety of your home.

5. When it comes to growing potted plants, friends all say that:
a) you've got a "green thumb."
b) you should consider being a florist.
c) your Chia pets are nice.

6. Mud, grass-stains, and wet weather
a) make you run for cover.
b) don't bother you.
c) are kind of fun, but can also ruin your clothes.

7. When it comes to plants, you
a) like the ones you can grow and eat.

b) like the idea of testing plants in order to find new uses for them.

c) think they're pretty things to have around.

Scoring:

1. a.3 b.2 c.1
2. a.2 b.3 c.1
3. a.1 b.2 c.3
4. a.3 b.2 c.1
5. a.3 b.1 c.2
6. a.1 b.3 c.2
7. a.2 b.3 c.1

17–21 points: Good for you! You aren't afraid of nature, you think it's beautiful and love to be a part of it. Let your enjoyment of nature guide you to learn more about the many different natural sciences. You might want to help protect and preserve our natural spaces for future generations to enjoy.

12–16 points: You like nature, but think it's a little too "wild." Sometimes you're even freaked out by how unpredictable Mother Nature can be. Well, since nature is a big part of this world we all live in, it's best to learn about it, experience it, and protect it. Ask your parents to take you on a camping trip and keep your eyes and ears open—it's a fantastic world out there!

7–11 points: Your idea of getting into nature is probably digging into a really big salad—with a fork and plenty of napkins. Come on! Explore a little, get some dirt under your fingernails, hold a bug in your hand. Sometimes you have to take a risk and try something new. Discovering nature can be an adventure!

The environmental sciences include ecology, botany, forestry, and agricultural sciences. These sciences deal with plants, animals, people, and other things that interact with the earth. An environmental scientist might examine a whole continent, or just one pond. Even your skin is an ecosystem for tiny organisms. Everywhere there is life, there has to be an ecosystem that supports that life. (Cities, for instance, are special ecosystems, because they are created by people rather than nature.) So if you're a nature lover, you may have a knack for environmental science!

Women Environmentalists

Women have been very influential in the field of environmental science. Before ecology was developed, people had studied plants, rocks, and animals, but no one thought of them as a system. Now, many scientists study the way ecological systems interact. The scientists who "founded" ecology started out in other sciences such as chemistry (Ellen Swallow Richards) and biology (Rachel Carson). These women changed the way people think about and treat their environment—revealing, for example, how chemicals affect wildlife and ecosystems.

Careers for the Environmentally Minded

Many environmental scientists get to work outdoors. They get paid to tromp around forests, explore wetlands, oceans, and rivers. Ecologists and environmental scientists can choose to specialize in their favorite kind of habitat, and then spend lots of time there—whether it's lush tropical coasts, ancient European vineyards, or wild Western mountains.

Ecologist: All the living things on the Earth—including people—affect the land, the air, the seas, and each other. By studying how plants, animals, and people interact with the earth, ecologists can help us maintain a landscape that we want to live in, and repair the ugly scars that careless people leave on the land and seas.

Horticulturist: Horticulturists study plants suitable for gardening and farming. They breed plants to create new, stronger varieties, and test different ways to keep plants healthy, suppress weeds, and keep pesky insects

Rachel Carson
1907–1964

"I can remember no time when I wasn't interested in the out-of-doors and the whole of nature."

"What's this?" young Rachel pointed to a tree she found in her backyard.

"That's a dogwood tree," her mother explained.

"What's this?" Rachel pointed again, to another tree.

"A maple tree," her mother said patiently. "And over there is an elm tree, and there's a cherry tree." Rachel looked all around her. It seemed like her mother knew everything about the nature in their backyard. Someday, Rachel thought, I'll know all the names of the living things around me, too.

Rachel Carson was born in 1907 in a small, rural town called Springdale, Pennsylvania. Whenever Rachel wasn't curled up with a book, she could be found in the backyard, spying on creatures and plants. Rachel's love of nature would provide the basis for her future creative and scientific careers.

As a girl, Rachel loved biology but also dreamed of becoming a writer. When she was only ten years old, *St. Nicholas'* magazine, a popular children's magazine, published her article, "A Battle in the Clouds," for which she received ten dollars. When she was older, Rachel decided to study English at Pennsylvania College for Women. But it wasn't long before a biology class reawakened her love of the natural world. Instead of English, Rachel decided to study zoology—the science of animals. She attended graduate school at Johns Hopkins University in Maryland to study marine biology—the life under the oceans. Rachel's studies led her to a career in marine biology. She was an expert in underwater life.

Rachel combined her talents for science and writing on a radio show for the U.S. Bureau of Fisheries, called *Romance Under the Waters*. She also wrote articles for magazines like the *Atlantic Monthly* on the fascinating life beneath the sea.

Remembering her own childhood lessons in the backyard, she wrote an article called "Help Your Child to Wonder," about the wonder and beauty of the living world around us. Rachel worked for the U.S. Fish and Wildlife Service for fifteen years, writing and learning, and eventually became the editor-in-chief of all their publications.

Rachel continued to write outside of work, too, publishing several books about the amazing and wonderful things that scientists study. *Under the Sea-Wind*, *The Sea Around Us*, and *The Edge of the Sea* were published between 1941 and 1957, all well-written histories of the ocean and how life began in the sea. By 1952, Rachel was 45 years old and was able to retire from her job and support herself by writing.

Rachel always hoped that nature would be around forever for other people to enjoy and study, but it became disturbingly clear that her hope was threatened. Rachel's friends told her about birds dying on their land after crops were sprayed with the insect repellent DDT. Scientists and wildlife watchers noticed that the chemicals in DDT killed not only bugs, but birds, fish, and other creatures living on the land. People using chemicals against insect pests didn't seem to care about the effects they had on other creatures.

So Rachel turned from writing about the beauty of nature to writing a book about chemicals that could harm wildlife. She wanted to write a book that would make people think carefully about the chemicals they used, and how these chemicals were affecting the environment.

The companies that made and sold the chemicals, and the scientists who researched and developed them, didn't want anyone to believe the message in Rachel's book, concluding that if people took Rachel seriously, the chemical companies would look irresponsible. They would lose business and might even be sued for the damages their chemicals caused. Although some of those scientists agreed with Rachel, they were afraid of losing their jobs if she used their names in her book. Before the book was published, the chemical companies began a media campaign attacking Rachel. They wanted the public to think that she was foolish.

People trusted Rachel more than they trusted the chemical companies, because she was a great writer and scientist. By attacking the book before it was even published, the chemical industry only succeeded in bringing more attention to the problem.

When Rachel's book, *Silent Spring*, was finally published, it became a huge bestseller. The book revealed the harmful affects of man-made chemicals on our environment. *Silent Spring* helped to encourage people to protect the land, and to inspire the government to pass new environmental regulations.

Unfortunately, Rachel died of cancer only two years after *Silent Spring* was published. Today, we know that many of the chemicals that Rachel warned against are "carcinogenic," or cancer-causing. Rachel may have been affected by exposure to the same chemicals she warned people about in her book. But within a few years of *Silent Spring's* publication, the Clean Water and Clean Air Acts were written, to help protect people from the careless use of poisons.

from destroying crops. They learn how to balance the needs of the garden and the soil.

Botanist: Plant scientists, also called botanists, study all sorts of plants—flowers, trees, shrubs, carnivorous plants, seaweed, wild edible plants, you name it! Botanists might do their research in a forest, meadow, farm, mountain, swamp, backyard garden, library, museum, or even undersea.

Ethnobotanist: Ethnobotanists study cultures all over the world, past and present, to see just how these cultures used plants to survive. Did they eat plants for food? Use them for shelter? Heal the sick? Many of today's modern medicines are discovered by studying plants that have been used for years by folk healers.

Environmental Consultant: When you build a new house, install power lines or roads, or tunnel under a riverbed, you need environmental consultants to tell you what to watch out for (like sinkholes in the soil), and how to make sure you don't harm natural resources.

Ecosystem Biologist: Ecosystem biologists go to unusual habitats, like wetlands, to study the plants and animals that make their homes there. They take note of the populations of certain animals, and of how the habitats are being affected by other animals.

Conservation Biologist: These scientists study and protect areas of land where unusual species grow. They might restore damaged land (like a trash dump) to its natural condition, or study pristine forests, hills, and swamps to document what animals and plants live together there.

Habitat Planner: Understanding how living creatures and plants interact is a great place to start when designing a living space—whether it's a zoo, park, house, or an entire city.

Entomologist: An entomologist studies insects. They may study agricultural pests, predator insects, and insects as food for other animals (including people!), or they might use insects as indicators to study other things—for example, entomologists might notice that a particular stream is unhealthy by looking at the amount of insects present.

Mycologist: Fungi and related microorganisms are the focus of a mycologist's study. Fungi aren't plants, they're a different kind of organism. Mycologists study everything from mushrooms to tiny germs that can grow on animals or plants.

How to Get Involved in Environmental Science

Going to school for environmental science means not only studying a lot of biology, ecology, or agriculture, but also taking chemistry, computer science, and technical writing. You can learn about specific areas, like plant studies (botany) or insect studies (entomology). You might also study agriculture, veterinary medicine, wilderness survival skills, and math subjects like statistics and chaos theory. These skills will come in handy when observing plants and animals in the wild.

Playing with Plants

Want to explore nature on your own? Try these experiments, indoors or out.

Blue Sunflowers? For this ecology experiment you will need to find a sunflower, a white daisy, or another light-colored flower. Put the flower in a large cup of water. Then dye the water with a little food coloring. Wait several days, adding water if it gets low. What happens?

Try this experiment with other flowers or colors. Do different flowers do the same thing? What happens in different conditions—a sunny place, shade, cool, heat?

Other plants may work, too—celery is a favorite, and it's fun to slice open afterwards and see where the color is inside the plant. Check it out with a magnifying glass if you like. You could even eat the celery for an after-science snack!

Backyard Biology: Ecologists often study biodiversity: how many different kinds of living things are in one area.

Check the biodiversity in your yard or playground with a "counting square." Tape together four rulers (or sticks) to make a square. Set your square down on the ground, and look for living things inside it. Grass? Flowers? Insects? Worms? List what you see, and how many of each kind. Drop your square somewhere else, and count again. Which areas have more biodiversity? Is there a reason? Count in other places, too—a friend's yard, a park, on vacation. Discover anything new?

Bug Bites: If you want to understand what a critter needs, try keeping it alive for a week.

Catch several live "bugs" of the same kind, and put them in separate containers. Give them the best "home" that you can. (Hint: Make it like the place where you caught them.) Don't forget to give all your captives water and air—carefully poke holes in the lid, or make a cloth cover instead.

To learn more about your captives, offer them something different in each container—maybe a new kind of food, or a shade-leaf. Do they eat it? Do they ignore it? What do your bugs like best? Once you're done studying your bugs, return them to the spot where you collected them and watch where they go.

Why Do You Love Science?

Surrounding us on all sides is immense beauty, often ignored, or passed by when we are in a hurry. It is not often that we take the time in our busy lives to touch the bark of a tree, feel the velvet of a rose petal, watch busy animals working hard to prepare for winter, or go out in the cold to watch the space station pass over our heads. Each part of our world is a thing of simple beauty, sometimes so small that no one notices. Yet the simplest part of our world, when explained from the perspective of science, suddenly becomes intricately complex and vitally important. In seventh grade, my science fair project involved testing car cleaners as watershed pollutants and for possibly harmful phosphate levels. My findings showed devastation to the watershed systems. Science forever holds fascination for me because there is an endless wealth of knowledge to be discovered.

—Elyse Hope, age 15

To me, science is like a puppy. Once you see how much fun it is you never want to stop playing with it. Science and technology are definitely my two favorite subjects. I am most interested in natural disasters. Ever since I saw the movie Twister, *I've been reading about tornadoes, earthquakes, volcanic eruptions, and flash floods. I would enjoy being a storm chaser. Another field of science that interests me is biology. I would also enjoy being a marine biologist or an oceanographer. In the seventh grade, I was involved in an after-school club called AWSEM. AWSEM stands for Advocates for Women in Science, Engineering, and Mathematics. I've been interested in science for as long as I can remember. All in all, science is a major part of my life, and it's part of who I am.*

—Meaghan Gallagher, age 13

Chapter 6

Not "Mad" Science: Chemistry

Your backyard fort is secretly a science laboratory, with jars of colored liquids and samples of slimy, sparkly concoctions. Mom finally got tired of the messes you made in the kitchen, tired of "potions" and volcanoes, and made you clean everything up once and for all. That's okay, because it gave you the idea of creating a "supercleaner" that could clean everything with just one squirt.

In chemistry, there's always something new. You get to discover the secrets inside everyday stuff. Chemistry is the closest thing to real magic in science. You can make substances appear and disappear, change them from one thing to another, perform fireworks tricks, and make crazy explosions.

Chemistry is the study of the properties and composition of materials. Modern chemistry uses the idea of different elements, or types of tiny building "blocks." Different combinations of elements make up all the material things that we can see, touch, and taste. Chemists use a chart called the periodic table to help organize their knowledge of these different elements. By examining the interactions of elements, chemists can learn to

Quiz—Are You a Chemist at Heart?

1. You think chemistry is:
a) a dangerous occupation.
b) the best way to learn what the world is really made of—if you don't mind getting a little messy.
c) something that happens when you meet the boy of your dreams.

2. When you see someone performing a magic trick, you:
a) try to figure out how it works.
b) ask the person performing the trick to tell you how it's done.
c) don't want to know the secret—you just enjoy watching it.

3. Your family orders pizza, and on the box top there is a refrigerator magnet. You take the magnet and:
a) toss it on the fridge.
b) wonder why it sticks to the fridge.
c) take it to the junk drawer and see what attaches itself to the magnet.

4. When an experiment requires you to wait for results, you:
a) drum your fingers on the desk wishing it didn't take so long.
b) check your notes while waiting to ensure that you've done everything correctly.
c) decide to go grab a bite to eat and check on your experiment later.

5. Learning about things you can't see:
a) intrigues you.
b) is all right, as long as it relates to something real.
c) creeps you out.

6. The idea of the "mad" scientist:
a) cracks you up because you think there is no such thing.
b) reminds you of your science teacher.
c) reminds you of Frankenstein.

7. When you come across an unknown substance, you:
a) try to figure out what it is and how it got there.
b) poke at it with a stick to see if it moves.
c) ask your mom to make your brother clean it up.

Scoring:
1. a.2 b.3 c.1
2. a.3 b.2 c.1
3. a.1 b.2 c.3
4. a.1 b.3 c.2
5. a.3 b.2 c.1
6. a.1 b.3 c.2
7. a.3 b.2 c.1

17–21 points: Way to go! Your mind enjoys being active: thinking, studying, and questioning. You think "mad scientist" is a cool job description and would love to get paid for experimenting all day. Now, if only you had your own laboratory . . . just don't accept any jobs in creepy old castles, OK?

12–16 points: You may not be a chemist yet, but you can appreciate good chemistry when you see it. Consider taking a chemistry class with a really good teacher, or just letting your own curiosity out to play. Ask more questions and find your own answers. Don't be afraid to ask for help, but don't let someone "help" you right out of your own experiment.

7–11 points: You can relax—there appears to be no "mad scientist" blood in your veins. You are calm, collected, disinterested . . . let's just say it—bored with chemistry! You might need to get out of the lab and learn about how chemistry connects to real life—try learning more about the research behind cooking, sports equipment, shampoo, or cars. Then you might have some motivation to learn more about this amazing science.

understand how they work together. If you like interesting experiments, transforming one thing into another, and studying things that are invisible to the naked eye, then chemistry could be your science dream.

Famous Women Chemists

One of the cool things chemists get to do is create or discover materials with properties that are almost unbelievable when they are first announced. Radioactive elements like radium were first discovered by Marie Curie and her team. (They still creep us out—how would you like to work in a lab where everything glowed in the dark?) Bullet-stopping "Kevlar" fabrics were invented at DuPont by researcher Stephanie Kwolec in 1965. Patsy Sherman, a research chemist for the 3M company, came up with "Scotchgard" waterproofing spray (first sold in 1956) after noticing water rolling off an accidental spill on someone's shoe.

Some chemical innovations by women have affected areas such as naval operations and gasoline refining. Navy wife Martha Coston patented signaling flares for ships in 1871, and her system was adopted by the U.S., France, and other countries. A widely used way to purify gasoline was invented by Roberta Nichols, who has three patents for flexible fuel vehicles—cars that can run on either alcohol or gasoline.

Chemistry Careers

Chemists study everything from fire to plants and insects, from poisons to new medicines to the digestion of ordinary food. Some chemists try to invent new substances that will work better—products like synthetic rubber, Kevlar, and hundreds of different kinds of slimes, paints, glues, and solvents. Other chemists design products for art and entertainment—like colors for film and photography, fun fabrics, tough new materials for skis, shoes, and sleeping bags, and more.

Chemists might do research in a lab—testing different amounts of a chemical, or investigating different combinations of chemicals to see what results they get—or chemists might start by working on paper, or with a computer to see what results are likely, and then ask another scientist to test

Irène Curie
1897–1956

"Science is the foundation of all progress that improves human life and diminishes suffering."

Many people have already heard about Marie Curie. She won two Nobel Prizes, one for investigating radioactivity and one for discovering the elements radium and polonium. She's the one who started the Curie Institute, where top scientists meet to study and discuss cancer and medical research. Madame Curie is one of the most celebrated scientists ever.

But did you know Marie's firstborn daughter, Irène, also won the Nobel Prize? If you count Irène's brother-in-law, too, that makes four Nobel Prizes in one family!!

Irène was born in France in 1897, the year after radiation was discovered. In 1903, the year her parents won the Nobel Prize, Irène started school. Nosy reporters tried to interview her about her parents' discoveries when she was only seven. Irène developed two personalities: friendly and loving with her family, but quiet and sometimes distrustful around strangers.

When Irène was nine, her father Pierre was tragically killed by a horse-drawn cart. For years after that, even mentioning her father made Irène sad, so the family didn't talk about him much.

To give her quiet child room to explore, and a break from French public schools, Marie started a home-school group for Irène and ten other children. These kids learned a different subject from each family, according to what they could teach best.

Irène and her mother became very close and could talk about almost anything; Marie treated her children with love and respect, and encouraged them to explore. Irène took after her father, both in intelligence and personality. That may have helped Marie to recognize and trust Irène's scientific abilities.

As a teenager, Irène learned to devour books in French, German, and English. She went to college for two years, but then quit school to work. She helped develop X-ray machines and then worked on the battlefields serving as a nurse radiographer in the first World War. Though only a teenager, she not only trained field doctors in the new X-ray technology, but helped convince them to use the strange new X-rays to help their patients. Irène was so successful that when the war ended, she received a medal for her work.

In 1918, Irène took a job as her mother's assistant at the Curie Institute. After working there for a few years, she earned her Doctor of Science degree with radiation experiments on alpha particles.

Irène remained quiet, even stiff, in public. She dressed unfashionably in loose, comfortable clothes. Her passions were scientific experiments. In 1924 Marie Curie hired a new assistant for the Institute, Frederic Joliot, a soldier without a science degree. As head assistant at the Curie Institute, Irène taught him the techniques for studying radiation. Frederic was charming, and handsome, but also a quick learner, and good at sensing the feelings and relationships of people around him. Though their personalities were almost opposite, Frederic and Irène discovered a common interest in science and in each other. They were married in 1926.

Their first child, Hélène, was born in 1927. Their son, Pierre was born next in 1932. Though plagued by health problems, Irène never complained. Antibiotics had not been discovered yet. More than a decade later, an antibiotic, streptomycin, would cure Irène's illness, tuberculosis.

After doing many important experiments, in 1934 the Joliot-Curies made their biggest breakthrough: they created tiny amounts of artificial radioactive materials from ordinary elements like aluminum. Normally, radioactivity occurs when big elements break down into smaller ones, spewing energy and little chunks of matter all over the place. But big, radioactive elements are pretty rare. The very next year, in 1935, Irène and Frederic won the Nobel Prize in chemistry for this achievement.

Radioactive isotopes, such as those the Joliot-Curies discovered, are still important today. For example, in medicine, small amounts of radioactive isotopes can be sent into a patient's body. Biochemists design special carrier molecules to take the radioactive isotopes to specific organs. When the radioactive element is concentrated inside one organ, the organ can be seen with an X-ray camera. This can help doctors diagnose problems without cutting the patient open.

Unfortunately, those that discovered radioactive material suffered from their exposure to it. When the Curies first started working with radiation, no one knew that it could cause cancer. Within months of the Joliot-Curie's most important discovery, Marie Curie died of the cancer leukemia. Marie was very excited about the artificial radiation experiment, but did not live to see her daughter and son-in-law win the prize.

So what did the Joliot-Curies do after they won the Nobel Prize? They built a tennis court at their new house, spent time together as a family, and continued to pursue their research. Fame brought rewards and reporters. Frederic became the head of an important research institute where he could work on nuclear physics, and later, head of the Atomic Energy Commission in France. Irène lent her name to political causes, like feminist organizations and anti-fascist movements, and took over her mother's position as head of the Curie Institute.

Irène would never become as famous as her mother—but perhaps fame was not what the shy, unconventional girl would have wanted. Growing up in a rich and exciting scientific environment, working on battlefields, running world-class laboratories, and raising a family of her own, Irène enjoyed the fruits of her parents' fame and encouragement.

Though Irène's long exposure to radioactivity harmed her body, her work healed many other people. Irène pioneered modern X-ray technology, and helped to develop it into the sophisticated tool it is today. She also joined France's Atomic Energy Commission, and worked to put the tremendous energy of nuclear fission to work as nuclear power. Today, France gets more of its energy from nuclear power than any other nation.

Irène Curie was one of the most influential scientists of her time, and she used her knowledge for the benefit of humankind.

their predictions. There are tons of careers in chemistry. Here are just a few:

Pyrotechnician: These chemists work with fire and powdered chemicals to make beautiful fireworks and freaky (yet safe) special effects and explosions. Well, mostly safe.

Biochemist: Biochemistry is the study of the intricate chemistry of living cells. Biochemists may research DNA, hormones, plant growth, or brain chemistry. As a biochemist, you might discover a cure for cancer, or develop medicines that can help fight other diseases.

Food Chemist/Nutritionist: Food chemists come up with new, safe, and tasty food combinations for snack companies and the food service industry. Nutritionists study how our bodies use the food, and how to feed ourselves to stay happy and healthy.

Analytical Chemist: These scientists work behind the scenes in a lab to figure out what stuff is made of. Often they analyze samples that other people are unable to identify—from gunk in a jet engine, to moon rocks, to dangerous chemical spills or airborne hazardous materials like asbestos.

Chemical Engineer: Chemical engineers have a hand in just about everything from your favorite nail polish to the cereal you had for breakfast. These chemists find (or invent) the right material for the job, from bubble gum to microelectronics. They learn to use chemicals to improve foods, fertilizers, and clothes, as well as the environment.

Environmental Chemist: Chemicals don't just disappear once you use them. They may go down the drain, only to reappear in a river, the ground, or even the air. You need chemical sleuthing skills to make a clean space for new buildings, wildlife, and people. Environmental scientists study how chemicals can affect our surroundings, and how to safely remove or clean up any chemicals that pose a problem.

Chemistry Teacher: Also known as mad science professor. They get to do all the coolest experiments over and over impressing kids each year and, at the same time, teaching them more about chemistry (and maybe discovering a thing or two themselves by accident).

Ways to Get Involved in Chemistry

To pursue chemistry you will need to be curious, be willing to practice other people's experiments, and learn how to design your own experiments as safely as possible. The excitement of chemistry is not in the explosions, but in the unexpected surprise at the end of long, patient work. Try taking a summer science class, or get a chemistry set. Ask your teachers to show you their favorite chemistry experiments—and to help you design your own safe, fun variations. Read about current chemistry experiments in science magazines and online.

If you have an original idea or an exciting new experiment, go for it. You can invent things, make money doing chemistry "magic" shows, teach people chemistry, or even publish your research in professional science journals before you're out of high school!

Most people study chemistry in school at first, and then develop their careers after college. As you get into high school or college, you'll want to try chemistry classes and internships, and visit universities with chemistry research programs to see what it's like.

Chemical Experiments

DO try this at home—just be sure to label your experiments, and warn your family!

Purple Potions: Cut some purple cabbage into little pieces, and soak them in hot tap water for about five minutes. The water should turn purple. This colorful "cabbage water" can tell you whether something is an acid or a base.

Pour a little cabbage water into small white cups or saucers. Add something different to each dish, and see if the cabbage water changes color. Try household stuff like baking soda, vitamin C, antacid tablets, soap, lemonade, shampoo, or tomato juice. (Before you try other things, check with your folks.) What colors do you see?

If the cabbage water turns pink or red, you've discovered an acid. Don't be scared—"acid" means "sour," like pickles or lemonade. Very strong acids are dangerous, of course, but you don't usually find them in your kitchen. If something is a base, it will turn cabbage water blue or green. Base is the opposite of acid. Bases are usually bitter and slippery, like baking soda. Strong bases are also dangerous.

If you mix acids and bases, they react and neutralize each other. Watch out for fizz! See if you can get the color to turn back to purple. Be sure to clean up afterwards!

Can you find another purple plant that changes colors? Try dark-colored flowers or berries.

Etch-an-Egg: Once you've identified some acids, like vinegar, here's another experiment you can do. Place a raw egg (still in its shell) in a cup of vinegar for two to three days. What do you think will happen? (Hint: Eggshell is mostly calcium carbonate, chemically similar to baking soda.) Would this work the same way with another acid, like lemon juice? Try it! Make sure to wash your hands after handling the egg.

Why Do You Love Science?

Science can be kind of creepy, but you can learn a lot by studying science. It's so amazing to learn about new things. In science there are also lots of experiments you can try, like mixing dry ice with water. But trust me, some experiments are better to do outside or in a science lab. I love to try new experiments! Science teaches everybody about nature and chemicals. You can also learn about frogs, snakes, pigs, and other animals, too! If you like science— take my word for it—you could even have your own laboratory one day. I love science! —**Josephine Rios, age 11**

I have always been one to ask the "how" and "why" questions about aspects of the world around me. There is always more to an object or event than meets the eye and, for me, science opens the doors to the fascinating intricacies of everyday things. For example, the colorful coatings of M&Ms are no longer just pretty, but can wonderfully illustrate chromatography, in a process of diffusing the dyes over silica powder to find the combination of pigments that produce the coating's colors. I enjoy science because it allows me to gain answers to my "hows" and "whys," prompts new questions that keep my mind active and curious, and lets me see everyday things in a new and interesting light. —Sara Manson, age 16

I've always been curious. I got interested in chemistry when my grandmother sent my older brother a chemistry set for his birthday. I watched my brother do experiments and I wanted to try. Chemistry is about using chemicals to make formulas. You mix the chemicals to make a reaction. It's exciting! When you combine two different chemicals, changes happen. My dad and I would mix powder and liquid chemicals in test tubes and keep them in a test tube holder in the basement. Every day I would go down to observe the reactions. Sometimes the powder would settle to the bottom of the test tube, sometimes bubbles would form and float to the top. Sometimes the chemicals seemed to steam or the liquids would change colors from blue to green. I really like to notice the changes. You can find out new things by observing. I really like chemistry. —Michelle Devoe, age 8

Chapter 7

Reaching for the Stars: Space Sciences

You're huddled under a blanket, hanging out on a lawn chair in your backyard. It's a perfect evening for stargazing. The moon is below the horizon and millions of bright stars dot the sky. You grab a book of constellations and look for your favorite, Cassiopeia. Whenever you can, you try to stay up late to watch meteors scrape their dazzling trails through the sky.

The night sky is beautiful, full of hidden depths and mysterious patterns waiting to be uncovered. Scientists love a mystery as much as anybody, and a mystery that involves the whole universe is a great one.

Space scientists are the lucky people who—you got it; study space. It's a fascinating job—you might earn your pay by doing experiments, like growing crystals and plants in microgravity, building and fixing satellites, testing tools and toys for future space missions, or creating and launching robots to explore deep space. You might live and work on a space station one day, or be the first human to travel to another planet. Sound exciting? Then read on.

Quiz—How Do You Know If Space Science Is for You?

1. When you look at the moon it makes you:

a) think of romance or haunted houses.

b) dream about going there someday to explore and collect samples. ✓

c) wonder why we only have one.

2. You tell your parents this summer you'd like to:

a) go to space camp.

b) go to your usual summer camp.

c) visit the planetarium.

3. As far as sleep goes:

a) you feel you need your full nine or ten hours for beauty and health.

b) you're a night owl, or you don't mind sleeping odd hours.

c) you don't mind staying up late on the weekends, but prefer normal hours during the week.

4. When you look at the stars, you:

a) wonder why some are brighter than others, and why they twinkle.

b) try to find the constellations.

c) get lost in space.

5. If you had the chance to go into space, you would like to:

a) explore to see if there is life on other planets.

b) take lots of pictures.

c) overcome your fear of heights while there.

6. If you were lost at sea and the radio didn't work, you would:

a) figure out what direction you needed to go using the stars and the angle of the sun.

b) send out an S.O.S. using smoke signals.

c) use your time to count the stars.

7. You're most comfortable working:
a) alone, atop a mountain.
b) in a crowded space or a tiny closet.
c) in wide open places with lots of room to move around.

Scoring:
1. a.1 b.3 c.2
2. a.3 b.1 c.2
3. a.1 b.3 c.2
4. a.2 b.3 c.1
5. a.3 b.2 c.1
6. a.3 b.1 c.2
7. a.3 b.2 c.1

17–21 points: Excellent! Did we catch you daydreaming about piloting the space shuttle, hanging weightless miles above the earth? Have we interrupted your search for the next new comet? You would enjoy a career in space science. If you'd like to be an astronaut, an astrophysicist, or an astronomer, you've got a good start. Never let gravity get you down!

12–16 points: Although you may not want to join the team at NASA any time soon, you appreciate the beauty and complexity of the universe. You have some good knowledge and skills so far, so keep learning. There is so much out there!

7–11 points: There's "space" in your head for a little more attention to space science. When you hear the word "stars," you think of Julia Roberts and Ben Affleck. Well, exit the movie theater and look up. There they are: billions and billions of beautiful lights—maybe the suns of other worlds like ours. Find out a little bit more about space—it's truly awesome.

Women Astronomers

Caroline Herschel made a name for herself in astronomy while helping her brother, William. Between polishing telescope mirrors and keeping house, Caroline helped with the observations that discovered the planet Uranus. Caroline alone found a total of eight new comets and many nebulae—the beautiful clouds of gas and dust in the universe that are the birthplaces of new stars. King George III of England was so pleased with Caroline's work he awarded her a stipend of 50 gold pieces a year for her discoveries.

Though William Herschel was a founding member of the Royal Astronomical Society in the 1820s, his sister was not. The Society was officially all-male for almost a century, though it began admitting "honorary" women members within a few years of its founding. Caroline Herschel and Mary Somerville were the first of these, in 1835. The King officially changed its charter in 1915, to include women and men, "without distinction of sex."

The world record for discoveries in modern astronomy is held by Carolyn Shoemaker. She beat Caroline Herschel by quite a bit—beat her by twenty-seven new comets! In the course of her career, Carolyn Shoemaker has discovered 800 asteroids, including some that were approaching the Earth (fortunately, all of them missed). Today, she works at the United States Geological Survey in Flagstaff, Arizona, and gets a few hours each week to point the massive Mt. Palomar telescope toward whatever corner of the sky she wants to see.

Careers in Space Science

Here are a few of the many different jobs that pertain to space science:

Astronaut: Astronauts can be from any scientific or technical background; what's special about them is that they go into space during part of their career. Examples include space shuttle pilots, navigators, and commanders, and "mission specialists" like engineers, biologists, teachers, doctors, photographers, or anyone else who is called to do a job in space. Many astronauts learn to do more than one job; being a good learner is important for becoming an astronaut.

Astronomer: The word astronomer means "naming the stars," but it includes much more than giving stars names. Astronomers also discover and name new planets, nebulae, black holes, and anything else that can be found beyond the Earth's immediate sphere. They study stars, galaxies, and deep-space supernovas (exploding stars), usually with telescopes, cameras, and detection devices that pick up light or radio waves.

Aerospace Engineer: These engineers design spaceships, or rockets, missiles, and satellites. Imagine trying to create something that can withstand the extremes of outer space and the harsh environments of other planets in our solar system.

Cosmologist: A cosmologist is someone who works to understand the universe as a whole: how it came to be, its history, and the rules of the galaxies, stars, and planets. After astronomers collect information about stars, comets, galaxies, and background radiation, cosmologists put it all together to tell the story of how our universe was born and what it's like, and sometimes to guess its future.

Astrophysicist: Astrophysicists use physics to study stars and other bodies in space. Their specialties include understanding how gravity, motion, light, and radiation work in space. Astrophysicists study the laws of the universe and try to predict freaky new discoveries like black holes. Sometimes they get to ride along on the space shuttle, too.

Astrobiologist: The science of astrobiology combines biology (understanding what life looks like), and astronomy and geology (understand information about stars and planets). Astrobiologists use tools from all these sciences to look for planets that could support life (or evidence of actual aliens!).

Aerospace Scientist: Aerospace scientists include engineers, technicians, chemists, and physicists who develop tools, fuels, and aerodynamic designs for airplanes, rockets, space vehicles, satellites, and other high-altitude technologies.

Observational Astronomer: This is a good job for people with keen eye-sight and patience for memorizing details. Observational astronomers, as the name suggests, observe (or watch) stars and other things in space. Most astronomers chart new areas of space, or use new technology (such as the Hubble Space telescope, infrared telescopes, and computer-aided charting systems) to gather more information about what's out there.

How to Get Started

So how do you go about getting into space? Since science research happens in space, it's a good idea to study some kind of science. Luckily, different types of science experiments are done in space, so you can pick whatever subjects you like best. Astronauts Millie Hughes-Fulford and Cady Coleman started out in chemistry, Sandra H. Magnus in electronics, and Chiaki Mukai in medicine.

If you want to study space flight, look for programs that include aerospace physics and engineering. To do astrophysics means working hard in math and physics. Col. Susan Helms and Col. Eileen Collins took a traditional path: they joined the Air Force and became pilots, and then got into the space program, just like the first astronauts. Aspiring astronauts often take flying lessons on the side to become pilots.

Whether or not you want to go into space, you might still enjoy watching it from Earth. Contact your local astronomy society or planetarium to learn about star parties or other astronomy events. Read up on black holes, quasars, and the Big Bang in science magazines. Check out NASA's Web site for the latest cool pictures from space. And if you ever need the real scoop on a starry rumor, try the International Astronomical Union.

Astronomy Adventures

Space is so vast, there's always room for another astronomer. Sometimes the best experiments happen when we allow ourselves to gaze at the ordinary.

Host Your Own "Star Party": Ask some friends to join you for stargazing on a clear night. Get a star chart, if you can (try your local bookstore or library). Gather flashlights, lawn chairs, bug spray, notepads, warm blan-

Mae Carol Jemison

1956–

"Each one of us has the right and the responsibility to live up to our individual potential and ambitions."

"Who knows what they want to be when they grow up?"

Five-year-old Mae raised her hand, waved it in the air, practically falling out of her seat. She knew the answer to this question. She waited impatiently while the teacher called on other kids. Finally the teacher pointed at her.

"A scientist!" Mae burst out.

The teacher gave her a confused look. "Don't you mean a nurse?"

"No," countered Mae indignantly. "I mean a scientist."

This would not be the last time Mae would have to defend her career and to prove she meant to become a scientist. Mae grew up in a time when few scientists were women, and even fewer scientists were African American. Mae was both, but this young girl living in inner-city Chicago was as determined as they come. She was going to be a scientist.

Seven years after her kindergarten teacher questioned her about her choice of profession, Mae had already decided that she would go to space. Never mind that at that time NASA would not accept women into the astronaut program. Only military test pilots—all men—were allowed to be astronauts. But by the time Mae saw the first man walk on the moon, she knew that she had to travel to space.

Fortunately, the world was changing. The original *Star Trek* debuted in 1966 and for the first time, an African American woman had a technical role on a TV series. Lieutenant Uhura, played by Nichelle

Nichols, became one of Mae's heroes. Nichelle Nichols would later help NASA recruit young women and minorities to the space program.

In high school, Mae worked hard. She became president of the student council, graduated at the top of her class, and was voted "most likely to succeed." She graduated early at the age of sixteen, and decided to leave her friends and family behind in Chicago to attend college in California, at Stanford University.

Mae found herself once again having to prove herself. She was one of only a few women in the engineering department. Mae dove right in, taking the required classes to get her degree in chemical engineering, and at the same time attending courses in African American studies. She learned to speak Swahili and got involved in student government. While in college, Mae traveled to Cuba and Kenya. After graduation, Mae went on to Columbia University's medical school in New York City.

In 1986 Mae decided to apply for NASA's astronaut program. But before she had a chance to turn in her application, tragedy struck; the *Challenger* shuttle exploded after takeoff, killing the entire crew. NASA decided not to recruit new astronauts until they could figure out what caused this horrific accident.

A year later, Mae heard from NASA again. She filled out her forms, and sent them in, never telling her friends that she was applying. She went to the Johnson Space Center in Houston for interviews and the required medical testing, and then went back home to Los Angeles. She waited. And waited. And waited. Finally, she got the call; NASA wanted her to be one of its astronauts!

How did Mae celebrate? By staying up late and watching old *Star Trek* reruns, of course.

Astronaut training was intense. Mae and the other astronauts had to learn about planetology (the science of planets), geology, meteorology, the history of human space flight, and the technical aspects of the spacecraft. They flew in supersonic jets and practiced space survival training.

After a year of studying and preparing for space flight, the astronauts were ready. On September 12, 1992, the space shuttle Endeavor lifted off from Kennedy Space Center in Florida. On board were seven astronauts, including Mae. The shuttle shot up 200 miles into the sky, where it began its orbit of the planet. The ship was going nearly 18,000 miles an hour, and went around the Earth 127 times in eight days. They had a complete science lab on board, in which Mae and the other scientists conducted experiments to see how they were affected by space and weightlessness.

While on board the Endeavor, Mae also used herself as an experiment, studying the symptoms of the motion sickness that many astronauts experience in space. With no gravity, no up or down, always being weightless, many astronauts end up with headaches, sinus congestion, vomiting, and fatigue. As a physician, Mae was used to recording symptoms and illnesses; however, this time she was her own patient! Mae wore a special uniform that monitored her body functions. She recorded her temperature, blood flow, and symptoms of motion sickness, and the methods used to make herself feel better. Mae's experiments helped future astronauts control their own motion sickness.

When Mae returned to Earth, the city of Chicago held a six-day tribute in her honor. She appeared on TV, and in parades, and made speeches to different groups, including her old high school. Mae eventually left NASA to teach courses in space technology at Dartmouth College in Hanover, New Hampshire. Today Dr. Mae Jemison, astronaut, physician, teacher, and businesswoman, lives in Houston, Texas. Always seeking new adventures, Mae created her own company called The Jemison Group, to help promote space technology and education in developing countries.

kets, and a thermos of hot chocolate (optional). Head out to your back-yard, or somewhere you can see the sky.

Lie back and gaze at the stars. Get comfy. Cover your eyes and count to sixty to adjust your night vision. How many stars can you see? Imagine "connecting the dots" to make shapes, like ancient peoples did. Describe your favorite constellations to your friends, and see if they can find them. You can use a star chart to learn the ancient constellations: try Cassiopeia, the queen (she's shaped like a "W"), and the Big and Little Dippers (they're near the North Star). Since the distant stars stay still, while the earth and planets zip around, astronomers use constellations to tell directions in space.

Time Tracking: The night sky changes from day to day and year to year. Write down what you see each night, and look for patterns. If there's only half a moon this evening, can you predict how soon there will be a full moon? Where's Venus tonight? What times of year can you see Orion?

Away from city lights, you can see much farther into the starry depths of the sky. Take a night ride to the countryside, or camp out. Would you like to see "shooting stars?" Ask your local librarian or astronomy society to help you find out when to look for meteors, planets, satellites, and other special stuff like comets and auroras. Some of the annual meteor showers are:

Jan 1–4: Quadrantids
May 2–7: Spring Aquarids
July 26–31: Summer Aquarids
August 10–14: Perseids
October 18–23: Orionids
November 14–20: Leonids
December 10–15: Geminids.

Why Do You Love Science?

I went outside and lay on a rock and looked up at the night sky. It seemed like the stars were so far away. To be that incredible distance and still shine down on us and light the sky is amazing. The stars, the constellations, the black holes, the comets, the entire solar system makes me wonder. How can the stars stay in their positions in the sky for such a long period of time? It's amazing to think that we're not the only planet in the universe and that there is a huge galaxy to explore. What would it be like to get up close to a sun or a star or travel into another galaxy? If you traveled into a black hole, where would it take you? I wonder about a lot of things. I wonder about leaves changing, the placement of stars, tornadoes, hurricanes, waves, waterfalls, rivers, and streams. Shouldn't the ocean overflow? Yet, it all comes around in a cycle. It's amazing! It's science!

—Sarah Schmidt, age 10

I have liked science ever since I was three, when my mom let me look through her telescope. I told her then that I wanted to be a doctor in outer space to heal aliens. At first I thought I would like to be a doctor, but now I like all science including astronomy, biology, chemistry, and more. I like science because there are questions that I've always wanted answers to, but may never find out. How did we get here, why are we here, and for how long? I guess maybe science makes me feel closer to answering those questions. I try to do a lot of experiments at home and at school, especially chemistry. I love gathering as much science information as I can. When I grow up, I would like to be a mission specialist in space; to be more specific—a chemist in space.

—Samantha Hansen, age 9

I've always looked at the stars and wondered about how distant they were, or what else was out there in the seeming oblivion. I'd always been the girl whose favorite channel was PBS. Who, once she entered school, would always be the one to point out that light was the fastest thing, that dinosaurs were millions of years old, and that water was two elements (a compound) not one. I dream of formulas to produce gravity wells and time warps in the few precious moments before sleep. As of late, my greatest ambition in life is to be an astrophysicist. As my physics teacher says, "Learning is a verb. You can't just sit by and absorb knowledge, you have to want it enough to find a way to get it."

—Ariel Shultz, age 16

Chapter 8

Figuring It Out: Physics and Engineering

You can balance anything on the teeter-totter, no matter how big or small. Your room is full of crystals that scatter the light into rainbows, and funky gadgets that you've rebuilt to work better. Amusement rides are your favorite form of entertainment—you love how the biggest rides at the fair can create free-fall, or make you stick to your seat, upside-down, with extreme G's.

Physics makes it possible for us to fly to the moon, make water dance with colored lights at night, sail around the world, or microwave popcorn while watching a video at home. Engineers create bigger and better buildings and bridges, safer toys, and faster and sleeker cars. Physics helps engineers know how high things should be built, how heavy they will be, and how long it will take you to get out from underneath if they fall over. Physics is important to success in designing, creating and using everyday objects.

Within engineering and physics, there are many different specialties, everything from making the next big roller coaster to designing your power toothbrush. The sciences of engineering and physics help us understand how to build things better and how the world works. Curiosity may keep you wondering, "How can they do that?" Through understanding physics and engineering, you can actually know.

Engineering Women

Engineering a new technology can be a power trip—literally. The pioneers who first researched electricity, lasers, and radiation had no idea how their work would affect the world—light bulbs, laser surgery, and X-rays are now considered part of our daily lives.

Many women have used their engineering knowledge to create amazing technology, or to journey "where no woman has gone before." When the engineer of the Brooklyn Bridge in New York City got sick, his wife, Emily Roebling, took over the job of building it. Today, there is a dedication on the bridge to this great woman, because she was a major contributor to one of the largest engineering projects in America's history. Another woman engineer, Donna Shirley, left a lasting impression through her creation of NASA's Mars Pathfinder rover, Sojourner. Shirley's invention investigated the surface of Mars for almost three months, outliving by more than ten times its actual expected lifetime. These two women are celebrated because of their creativity and determination within the engineering world. (Look up the original "Sojourner Truth" for the story of another amazing woman—though she wasn't an engineer, her words have powerful inspiration for all of us.)

Careers in Engineering or Physics

Some of the following jobs use physics and engineering directly; others use the reasoning and problem-solving skills that you develop with science and math. If you are interested in engineering or physics, you might work in research and development, industry, finance, computer science, or medical

Quiz—Is Physics for You?

1. Your sister won't go on the newest roller coaster at the theme park, so you:
a) try to explain how it works, hoping to make her less scared.
b) ask the person running the ride if anyone has ever fallen off, proving to your sister that the ride is safe.
c) go on a smaller ride with her, to demonstrate that the rides are fun!

2. While playing basketball with your brother, you get into an argument. He thinks that if he keeps pumping the ball with more air, it will go higher. You:
a) go get the instructions, pointing out the place where it says not to pump too much air.
b) let him keep filling it up until it eventually pops. Otherwise he'll never learn!
c) explain to him about optimal pressure and the consequences of putting too much air in.

3. While you're babysitting, you spend time entertaining the kids by:
a) constructing a model city out of Legos.
b) finding new ways to play with their old toys.
c) popping the latest Disney movie into the DVD player.

4. Your cousin's coming to town. You want to take her to try some of your favorite things, including:
a) pool, pinball, ping-pong, or handball.
b) extreme carnival rides.
c) a magic show put on by you and your lovely assistant.

5. While at the beach one summer day, you:
a) try to time the waves so you don't get knocked over.
b) build the most elaborate sand castle ever.
c) pull out your binoculars and try to convince your sister that she can see China through them.

6. You hear the words "time travel" and you think that:
a) you'd like to use it to save the world.

b) it makes for good science fiction movies.

c) it would be cool to figure out if it's possible.

7. Your teacher launches into rocket science, and you think you missed something. You're confused about the assignment. You:

a) raise your hand, and make the teacher explain it again.

b) try to do the experiment anyway, and figure it out for yourself.

c) get together with your friends to try and puzzle out the homework together.

Scoring:

1. a.3 b.1 c.2
2. a.2 b.1 c.3
3. a.3 b.2 c.1
4. a.3 b.2 c.1
5. a.3 b.2 c.1
6. a.2 b.1 c.3
7. a.3 b.1 c.2

17–21 points: Wow! Impressive! You know enough about physics to explain your work to your friends and family. You probably love engineering and use it to solve everyday problems. Don't lose sight of common sense as you study—sometimes the simplest solution doesn't involve any equations at all.

12–16 points: You're getting there! You know that physics and engineering are important sciences that apply to lots of things we do and make. You've got a good start; keep up the momentum, and you'll be heading for a deep understanding of these important sciences.

7–11 points: When it comes to solving problems, physics is not the first thing that comes to mind. You're a good problem-solver, though, and that skill will help you learn anything you put your mind to. Keep trying and exploring. Once you figure something out for yourself, everything else seems more exciting. Once you know you can do it yourself, then you can choose whether to study more, or not.

applications. Your employer might be a school, a research institute, a hospital, the military, a government agency, or a private company. Engineers are given some of the most puzzling problems in the world to solve. They use science and their problem-solving skills to come up with new ideas and solutions to make things work.

Computer Engineer: When you are surfing the Internet, you are using technology created by computer engineers. Computer engineers are always trying to improve the performance and efficiency of the computers we rely on. Currently, they are working on designing computers with smaller cases, flatter screens, and faster processors that will go with you to school or fit in the palm of your hand.

Civil Engineer: Civil engineers are responsible for the roads we drive on, the bridges that span large bodies of water, and the tunnels that travel under them. They design railways, mines, and buildings that are important parts of our communities and economy.

Electrical Engineer: As the name implies, electrical engineers work with equipment that disperses and conducts electricity. This could mean anything from cell phones to electrical wiring in buildings, from navigation systems to communications systems.

Chemical Engineer: These engineers come up with new materials, like plastics, Kevlar, and fabrics like Orlon. They also use chemicals to create new drugs that can fight diseases.

Toy Engineer: Toy engineers come up with blueprints for toy designs. That almost-completely-lifelike robotic cat (it meows and purrs) you designed could be all the rage next Christmas season.

Agricultural Engineer: Get in touch with your environment! As an agricultural engineer, you might be working on irrigation systems for farms or developing better ways to treat and recycle waste.

Physical Engineer: Physical engineers figure out how high a bridge can be raised, how hot the wires in your phone might get, and how to make things strong, heavy, light, hard, and flexible enough to do their jobs well.

Atomic, Nuclear, and Particle Physicist: These scientists study the tiniest particles of stuff that anyone can find, such as atoms and their nuclei, and the astonishing things that happen when you mess with them. They deal with huge amounts of energy, forces that are inconceivably strong, and tiny spiraling particles such as "quarks" with names like "strange" and "charm."

Biophysicist: These scientists use physics to study life. They may analyze the strength of bones, the dynamics of flight in birds, and the physical behaviors of joints and organs.

Construction Engineer: This kind of engineer can figure out the best way to construct a building, what materials to use to make it safe in case of earthquakes and hurricanes, and how to make it more energy efficient.

Physics Educator: Sharing the cool and important parts of math and science can take place in universities, colleges, high schools, elementary schools, or public science programs. An educator in physics may also write books; and talk to friends and kids.

Getting Physical

Like most sciences, the best way to get into these fields is to try some hands-on research and experimenting. You will get to do this if you take physics, engineering, or drafting classes in school. You may also want to try a summer job at an engineering firm, or maybe job shadow someone who has an interesting job already in physics or engineering. You might learn a couple of fun "How did they do that?" facts. Of course it's easy to observe physics and engineering in action in everyday life, too. Next time you're on a teeter-totter or on a bridge, just think about what you're learning!

Chien-Shiung Wu

1912–1997

"There is only one thing worse than coming home from the lab to a sink full of dirty dishes, and that is not going to the lab at all."

"Ignore the obstacles . . . just put your head down and keep walking forward," Chien-Shiung's father said to her. He knew his daughter, whose name meant "strong hero" in Chinese, would need a lot of determination in her journey to become a scientist, especially in a time when most scientists were men.

Chien-Shiung Wu was born near Shanghai, China in 1912. Education was important in her home—her mother was a school-teacher and her father founded the first school for girls in the area. Chien-Shiung excelled at her studies, and when she was ten she went away to boarding school, where she was at the top of her class.

At the age of eighteen, Chien-Shiung attended the National Central University in Nanjing to earn her degree in science, then decided to further her education in the United States. Leaving her family behind, Chien-Shiung made the trip to America on her own. In 1936 she started attending college at the University of California at Berkeley.

In 1937 all contact with her family in China was cut off. Japan invaded China and Shanghai came under Japanese rule. Chien-Shiung's parents could not contact her, and could no longer pay her tuition for college. Fortunately for Chien-Shiung, UC Berkeley awarded her scholarships that would pay for her classes and housing. These opportunities and her dedication to science made staying at school a better choice than returning home to a war-torn China. Sadly, Chien-Shiung would never see her family again.

By the time Chien-Shiung received her Ph.D. in physics, she was already known as an expert in the area of nuclear fusion. She began teaching at Smith College, a women's college in western Massachusetts, helping other young women pursue science.

During World War II, Chien-Shiung was invited to join the Manhattan Project. This secret project's goal was to create the first atomic bomb. Her expertise helped scientists better monitor radiation and beta decay, important factors in any nuclear experiment. After the war, when the project was over, she continued teaching and doing her own experiments.

In 1956 Chien-Shiung performed an experiment that caused quite a stir in the world of physics. She disproved a law of physics! She found that the laws of nature were not always symmetrical, as had been believed (called the conservation of parity). By monitoring radioactive cobalt in a lab, she was able to observe in which direction electrons were ejected. According to the theory, they should be ejected equally in opposite directions, but Chien-Shiung saw that this was not true. The electrons had a tendency to go in one direction.

Two scientists working in the field, Tsung Dao Lee and Chen Ning Yang, decided to duplicate this experiment, to see what Chien-Shiung had seen. In 1957, Lee and Yang were awarded the Nobel Prize in physics for this finding. To her disappointment, Chien-Shiung was not included, though she had been instrumental in making this important discovery.

She eventually became a professor at the prestigious Columbia University and was awarded the National Medal of Science, one of the highest honors for scientists. She also became the first woman to head the American Physical Society (in 1973) and the first woman to receive an honorary doctorate from Princeton University (in fact, she had honorary degrees from ten different universities!). By the time Chien-Shiung died in 1997, she had amassed quite a few awards and distinctions. She forged ahead in a field where very few women had gone, and the work she did is still important today.

Experimenting in Engineering and Physics

Hot Physics: Find a plastic two-liter soda bottle with its cap, and clean it out. Pour in a cup of very hot tap water (be careful). Shake the water around to warm up the whole bottle. Now get ready to trap warm air inside: quickly, pour the hot water out of the bottle, and then screw the cap on tight.

What happens as the air inside the bottle cools? What if you put it in the fridge? Why? Does it work the same way with warm or cool water? Often, things change size when they change temperature. Could you measure, or predict, how things change with heat? Can you find other things that expand and contract this way? Careful—don't try breakable things like glass.

Can you use this idea to make something move? How about making a temperature-detector? Consider hot-air balloons, and thermometers.

Engineering: Imagine a weird problem that involves physical objects. For example: How could you carry breakable eggs on a bicycle?

Can you solve the problem using things that you already have?

Look around your room for parts to work with. Sketch your design or idea. Think about things like safety (don't crash your bike!) and expense (would you spend $5 to protect $3 worth of eggs?).

Engineers like to make good ideas better. How could you improve your bicycle egg-carrier? Make it stronger? Faster? Smaller? Could you use it to carry other things, like a pet?

Why Do You Love Science?

One day my physics teacher decided to inform us that we would be building a nuclear submarine. Yes, there was no mistake; we would be designing and presenting a nuclear submarine in front of well-known marine engineers. We took a bus to the Merchant Marine Academy. When we finally reached our long-awaited destination, we went inside and were lectured on mysterious subjects. After the lecture we were taught about the mechanics of a submarine, and different metals and materials. The next day we found out what department we were placed in. I was in the nuclear reactor department. We worked very hard. After a long year of challenging physics it was time for our presentations in front of the marine engineers. I was able to give a convincing performance. I will never forget my physics teacher. He taught me very important skills and inspired an interest and excitement in science that I am sure will last throughout my life.

—Antonia Sohns, age 15

Have you ever wondered why a slinky walks down the stairs or why water stays in a bucket when you spin it upside down? I didn't know the answers to these questions either, until I got interested in science. Once when I was little, my mom bought me a slinky. I dropped it down the stairs to find that it walked for itself, and from then on I started learning about science. Aren't we glad that scientists study physics, because without physics most toys wouldn't even exist! Not only would toys not exist, also many other things like roller coasters, ferris wheels, and cars wouldn't be here today. Not only do these things involve physics, but also over a million different objects in this world do, too. I'll bet you could think of a bunch if you tried. I know I could.

—Tory McKnight, age 9

Chapter 9

The Mother of It All: Invention and Innovation

You would rather invent a new way to do your chores than get them done. Quickly, you brainstorm and attempt to come up with a creation that can save both time and effort. Nobody can quite figure out what your latest new gadget is, but they all agree that it looks cool.

One of the best feelings in the world is coming up with a really good idea. Inventing is something people naturally do all the time. Early humans invented what they needed to survive, to live together, and to feel at home in many different environments. Some of the cleverest inventions are so useful now that they seem obvious—but this happened only after someone had invented them. These inventions might have seemed weird or unnecessary at first. Imagine how people reacted to the wheel or the toothbrush when they were first invented. Today, it would seem strange if someone didn't use a toothbrush.

Inventing involves using knowledge from all different fields—from biology, physics, even art—to make or do something a new way. An invention is any useful new discovery—whether it's a machine or an idea for a better way to do something. Anyone can be an inventor; all it takes is just a great idea.

Women Inventors

Through the ages, women have invented tools to help them handle common tasks and daily chores. Today, many such women are employed by big research firms, but some have founded their own companies, profiting from their inventions. When artist Bette Graham, a single mother, had to start working again in the 1950s, she wasn't a perfect typist. She thought, "Why can't we paint over mistakes like artists do, instead of making a whole new copy because of one typo?" She invented a liquid correction fluid, "Mistake-Out" (later known as Liquid Paper), and went into business.

When Mary Anderson patented the first practical windshield wipers in 1905, many drivers thought little waving rubber blades in front of the driver would be too distracting. As more people started driving, windshield wipers became a standard option, and today no one would consider driving without them.

Women have invented fashion accessories, such as perfumes, jewelry, and devices and techniques for doing hair. The first permanent wave machine (for hair "perms") was patented by Marjorie S. Joyner in 1928. Majorie worked for African American hair entrepreneur Madame Walker, who had gone into business with a softener for black hair.

Innovative Careers

The sky's the limit when it comes to careers in inventing. New ideas are important in almost any job. They're needed in every field, whether it's science, business, art, or manufacturing. If you like the idea of inventing, you might be interested in the following careers:

Entrepreneur: An entrepreneur creates a new business, often to sell a newly invented service or product.

Quiz—Are You a Future Inventor?

1. Your toaster is broken, so you can't make that peanut butter toast you were craving for breakfast. You:
a) think of a way to use some skewers and the stove and toast away!
b) you warm up the bread in the microwave—at least it's hot, right?
c) decide that now is a good time to try your hand at making French toast.

2. Your little brother has taken your calculator and pulled it to pieces. You:
a) put it back together so it works—sort of.
b) show him how to put it back together.
c) leave it on your mom's desk. It's the perfect excuse not to do your homework.

3. You have the lead in the school play. Five minutes before your big scene, your pants split down the middle. You:
a) ask your teacher for a safety pin, and make sure you keep your back to the wall.
b) fashion a new skirt out of a nearby curtain.
c) start thinking about how to design a better pair of pants that won't split again.

4. The Science Fair is coming and you don't have a single idea for a project, so you:
a) go to the library and research a topic that catches your interest, then try to base your project on the topic.
b) set up your sister's project from last year and try to improve it.
c) pick five random objects from your room and make them into something.

5. You and your friends have one weekend to finish that giant group project for class and you keep getting stuck. You:
a) ask your dad, your teacher, the mailman, the guy at the ice cream shop, and anyone else who will listen for help.
b) start the project over, trying a new approach that might be more successful.
c) stay up all night drinking Mountain Dew until an idea comes to you.

6. Your favorite invention is:
a) a bicycle . . . or maybe a clock . . . anything with gears!
b) the double-scoop waffle cone with extra toppings.

c) a DVD or CD player—you're fascinated by anything that uses mini laser beams to transmit information and entertainment.

7. When you get a new gadget, the first thing you want to do is
a) find out how it works (and take it apart, if necessary!).
b) see if you can use it to solve a pesky problem you've been having.
c) tell the company who made it how they could make a better one. v· 3

Scoring:
1. a.3 b.1 c.2
2. a.2 b.3 c.1
3. a.1 b.3 c.2
4. a.2 b.1 c.3
5. a.1 b.3 c.2
6. a.2 b.1 c.3
7. a.1 b.2 c.3

17–21 points: You've already got a prototype for a flying car in your basement, right? You look around and see how things can be improved to work better, or how a different device would do the job faster. You take risks and learn from your mistakes. Inventing something is so exciting and fun that you dream of making it your career. Good luck!

12–16 points: You're starting to see how creative and exciting inventing can be. You like to create things, but you need to take more risks. It's okay to make mistakes, to make something that doesn't work at all, because that's how invention helps us learn. Taking risks makes success all the more satisfying.

7–11 points: So—you'd like things to be different, you appreciate improvements, but you don't really care much about how it happens. You find that it's just easier to let someone else solve problems, create new products, and make new discoveries. Challenge yourself to invent something new and unique—even if it's something only you would love. Nobody else can make as much difference in your life as you can!

Market Researcher/Consultant: These specialists gather information about what kinds of products people want. Market research helps businesses design and sell products that people would be interested in buying.

Product Tester: Product testers make sure that inventions actually work as intended. This job can be a lot of fun—you may get to break items on purpose, and get paid for it. And you get to play with new products before they are available in stores.

Product Designer: Designers usually work on coming up with new looks and shapes for products, like for fashion or furniture.

Technology Specialist: These researchers specialize in making custom tools for specific purposes, like manufacturing or scientific research. Sometimes you have to invent a whole new tool or machine to get a job done in the first place. Other times, you're trying to shave seconds off the processing time for cheese slices, sport shoes, or glow-in-the-dark stickers.

Things to Do to Become an Inventor

Though there are some schools with workshops for inventors, inventors historically have a reputation for being self-starters. Practice inventing at home—solve your own problems with creativity, adapt or redesign things to serve a different purpose. Get involved in "invention conventions," which are like school science fairs, but for inventions. Invite friends to play invention games like those listed at the end of this chapter.

Consider whether you would want a regular paycheck, or to be your own boss. If you're going to work in a company as an inventor, you might need some training in materials science or technology; if you're going to market your own inventions, some business education or marketing skills might come in handy, too.

But most of all, pay attention to things around you. School. Math. Geography. Science. Art. Music. Languages. You never know when a stray fact may connect with another thought, creating an opportunity for a new invention.

Margaret Knight (1838-1914) and the "Lady Edisons"

"As a child . . . the only things I wanted were a jack-knife, a gimlet, and pieces of wood."

For a simple invention, consider the humble brown paper bag. ("Is that even a real invention?") you might ask.) It might seem simple, but people didn't always have bags that could stand up by themselves. A cheap, quick way to make paper bags with flat bottoms was one of the inventions that made Margaret Knight rich and famous.

Margaret Knight didn't build a whole career on one paper-bag machine, though. She came up with almost a hundred different inventions—and put her name on thirty patents. Margaret Knight was one of the "Lady Edisons" who helped to invent the machines of the industrial age.

The "Lady Edisons" of the late 1800s and early 1900s included Knight, Beulah Henry, Helen Blanchard, and the unfortunate "Mary S." (Mary S. sold her ideas to men for as little as $5 instead of getting her own patents, and as a result stayed poor throughout her life.) The first three women made money for themselves by patenting hundreds of ideas: machines, methods, and small improvements to industrial and household devices. Some examples include sewing machines and techniques for making shoes and hats, a vacuum freezer, surgical needles, color-changeable umbrellas, and more. Each of these women created dozens of small inventions, getting comfortably rich but never quite famous.

The "Lady Edisons," not surprisingly, also created lots of products that have feminine appeal, such as clothes, sewing products, household conveniences, and fashion accessories. The bra was created by socialite

Mary P. Jacob in 1913 on her way to a party—the stiff wires of her corset wouldn't fit under her party dress.

Josephine Cochran, another society hostess, got tired of hearing dishes break in the kitchen and invented a dishwasher that actually worked. The device was so popular with her friends that she founded a company to produce them for homes, hotels, and restaurants. At the 1893 World's Fair, she won the highest award for her innovative machines. Her company is now known as KitchenAid.

The "Lady Edisons" of the 1800s were famous for adapting the technology of the day—machines, electricity, mass-produced clothes and household items. The most famous inventions of the 1900s were mostly chemical—Nylon, glow-in-the-dark paint, Teflon, X-rays. What will be the most famous inventions of the next century? Get in on the action early, and your name could be the one we remember.

Inventing Inspiration

Get some friends together to boost your creativity. Try these ideas:

The Mysterious Artifact: Take an ordinary object and pass it around. Pretend you've never seen anything like it before. Take turns "guessing" something weird it could be used for. For example, if you pass around a shoe, it could be "a play-house for a mouse," "a string-stretcher," "a really smelly lunchbox," "a cat toy," "something to throw at enemy tarantulas," or "wearable money." See how many different purposes you can come up with. (Silliness is encouraged.)

Variation: Take something "useless," like paper tubes or plastic bottles, and play the Mysterious Artifact game. Then see if you can make the "useless" object into something useful or fun.

Target Troubles: Brainstorm a list of "problems"—from serious stuff like world hunger to annoying stuff like leaky faucets or stinky leftovers. Once you have a good long list, see if you and your friends have any ideas to solve some of these problems. (Bonus points if you invent something to solve more than one problem at once!)

Invent-A-Thon: Give local inventors a chance to strut their stuff. Host an invention convention, fair, club, or contest. Invite your friends and neighbors to come see your stuff, and show off their own ideas. You can even "invent" ingenious prize categories so that everyone gets a prize. (Like a "Rube Goldberg" prize for the most complicated invention for doing something simple.)

Owning Your Ideas

You can probably imagine mechanical inventions, like toasters or electrical can-openers. But did you know that a recipe is also an invention? Inventions that can be protected by legal patents include not just machines, but also formulas for chemicals, foods, and drugs, and methods for doing certain things. Somebody has even patented a "method of exercising a cat" that involves wiggling a laser pointer in front of a cat to make it chase the red light.

To get a patent, you must apply for one through the Patent and Trademark Office (http://www.uspto.gov/). It can be a lengthy (averaging about two years) and expensive process to get a patent. You don't need a patent to sell your invention, but it will insure that no one else can steal your idea. There is no age restriction on getting a patent. In fact, the youngest person ever to get a patent was a four-year-old girl from Texas. Her patent was for an aid for grasping round knobs.

Why Do You Love Science?

I've always wanted a dog. I would like to invent something to help people understand dogs more. My invention would be something to help you understand what your dog is saying when he barks. It would be shaped like a Palm Pilot, and it would translate dogs' barks. Maybe it could be used to find out what your dog's body language means. If your dog was hungry or wanted more attention, you would be able to tell. For one thing, dogs would be happier. I might also like to be a canine detective. The science of criminology interests me. I would like to help in disaster areas, with kidnapping or even finding a missing pet. I would like to do these things because it would help our country. I enjoy animals, inventing, and scientific research. There are all different ways to do science and be in contact with your favorite things. —Emily Maroni, age 8

I've loved science ever since that fateful day in second grade when we had to study dinosaurs. Now that was a great day. Suddenly, my eyes were opened to a new way of life. Instead of wondering why a light bulb turns on whenever I flip a switch ten feet away, I could look it up in a book and understand the whole process. One reason I'm devoted to science is that I need to challenge my mind. I need to exert my tiny neurons to the fullest. It's a lot like working out. In fact, I've discovered that a hard-working mind does have positive results. I notice that I focus easier and get bored less often when my mind is being challenged. I do this in many ways, but science is a natural choice because it is a diverse, complex, ever-changing subject with many connections to daily life. You can see now why I am obsessed with science! —Bryn Cram, age 15

Chapter 10

Resources for the Science Savvy

There are a lot of different reasons that people study the sciences: to learn about beautiful or powerful things, to make money, to protect loved ones from a horrible disease, or to understand the life around us. Whatever your dreams in life, science can help you achieve them. It gives you power to understand your world, and helps you solve problems that might otherwise keep you from achieving your goals.

The greatest thing about science is that you get to choose where you want to go, and which mysteries you want to solve. Learning to answer your own questions is a skill that you can use your whole life. Anyone can do science. It just takes practice. Even if you decide not to become an astronaut or wildlife biologist, science will help you think and look at the world critically. Rather than believing everything that everyone tells you, you can judge for yourself if they make sense, or if they are just telling you a bunch of baloney.

Why does it make a difference if girls do science? Girls may have the best chance at the next big achievements in science. Achievements in science often come from people asking new questions. New questions lead to new discoveries, or new solutions to problems that were previously overlooked. Since there are more guys than girls in science, some questions important to girls may not get asked.

Luckily, there are lots of girls and women in science today. More women than ever before are becoming doctors, professors, technicians, engineers, mathematicians, science writers, and other scientists. These interesting women are working to cure diseases like cancer, studying the environmental effects of chemicals, designing better computer programs, and making other important discoveries.

There are whole fields of science today that didn't exist a hundred years ago—such as computer science, genetic engineering, and space research. Who knows what scientists will discover and study in another century? We hope that after reading this book, you'll discover enough great science to keep your mind dancing for the rest of your life.

What's Next?

So what do you do, now that you think you might want to be a scientist? Stick with it and keep exploring! Here are some tips.

Surviving Science Education

Sometimes school can be tough or boring. Don't let a bad experience kill your love of science. Here are some tips to help you have fun even in the most frustrating environments:

Nail-Biting Test Anxiety: Give yourself some credit for doing your best. One weird difference between guys and girls in science classes is that guys may act like they're doing OK even when they're not, while the girls often worry that they're flunking even when they're doing fine. So relax, already. Wait until you see the test scores before you rethink your whole life.

The Buddy System: Another thing that makes a big difference for girls and women in science is friends. Some guys seem happy to compete all the time, but some of us prefer to work together. So make some good girl-friends who will support you in your love of science. Simply hanging out with friendly, smart kids who share your interests can make it a lot easier to keep your dreams in mind.

Homework and projects can be more fun with a friend. Don't cheat, but help each other "get it." Two minds are sometimes better than one. You can come up with great ideas when you're talking to someone about it.

Family Chat: Families are a huge influence on scientists. You might have scientists in your family—birdwatchers, model-train hobbyists, teachers, or professional researchers. Get to know them.

Whether or not your family is science savvy, let them know that their support will encourage you to explore on your own. Ask your family for help if you're stuck or discouraged.

Tough Stuff: When things get hard, guys learn that they're supposed to "tough it out." Girls can "tough it out," too, but people don't always expect us to try. We can do it! So what are you afraid of? (It's also OK to cry when you're frustrated, or to ask for help.) Stick with your goals, even if you get upset, and make sure you keep learning from everything you do.

How to Find Out if Science is for You

Try It: There are lots of opportunities for you to explore science before you choose a career. Try a summer camp or weekend academy. Hook up with a mentoring organization like AWSEM (Advocates for Women in Science, Engineering and Mathematics) or the Girl Scouts. Volunteer for local nature programs, museums, or labs. Start an after-school club, or join activities like science and math contests. We've included a lot of resources at the end of this chapter to help you find or create these kinds of opportunities.

Talk to Real Scientists: Interview some local ones for the school paper. Ask your parents and teachers to help you recruit a panel for a career day at your school. Talk to scientists you already know: the teachers at your school, your doctor or dentist, the folks at the zoo. Ask them what their job is really like, how they got where they are, what they would recommend or do differently themselves.

This book is meant to give you an introduction to the exciting things you can do with science. There are many excellent sources out there for you to explore further. The Web sites we've included will help you find out more about science careers, organizations, and other famous scientists. You're never too young (or old) to get involved in science, and the following section will show you how to get started with science today!

Careers in Science

Wonderwise: Women in Science Learning Series
wonderwise.unl.edu

This Web site is loaded with great information for a girl interested in science. You can find biographies of women who are out in the world solving the problems that plague us every day. There are also activities that help you understand what the scientists are doing to help us live better lives.

National Institute for Environmental Health Sciences
www.niehs.nih.gov/kids/home.htm

This site has information for kids interested in science careers and also science project help.

Women in Mining
www.womeninmining.org

Have you ever wondered how the fireworks on the Fourth of July get to be those brilliant colors? Then this site is the one you want. It has great mineral-related activities, including a cake excavation idea, making toothpaste and cookies, and "mining" birdseed. Be sure to tell your teacher about this site so you can share some of these awesome activities with your classmates. There are links to other sites where you can get even more information about minerals and mining.

Girlstart
www.girlstart.com

On this Web site, girls can dive into their own world of math, science and technology. In the Science Circuit you can find out why a penny turns green or where ocean breezes come from. There is a chat room and cool experiments for girls who really want to do some great hands-on science.

Expanding Your Horizons (EYH)
www.twistinc.org

This non-profit organization holds conferences all over the nation for girls of middle-school age. At each conference you can attend science or mathematics workshops taught by women in the field. A real doctor will show you how to read X-ray charts and an archaeologist will show you how to reconstruct ancient pottery. EYH is focused on keeping girls interested in science and mathematics all the way through high school.

Real Science
www.realscience.org

This site is made for teens who have the desire to learn more about careers in science. There is an enormous list of all the different types of scientific careers. You can click on one that sounds interesting and you will find an interview with a scientist in that field and more helpful information.

Careers in the National Aeronautics and Space Administration
kids.earth.nasa.gov/archive/career

Almost everyone has wanted to be an astronaut. Some people have never outgrown that desire. This Web site shows those who still have a passion for space exploration and the different career paths that they can pursue at NASA.

USDA Agricultural Research Service
www.ars.usda.gov/is/kids/scientists/scientistsframe2.htm

On this site you can find information on many different careers in science. It even has a quiz that you can take to find out which career suits you best. You can get help on your homework assignments from Dr. Watts, but don't wait until the last minute. The main site, called Sci4kids, also has a ton of great information on almost anything you could think of.

Science Camps, Contests and Organizations

Computer Camps
www.microweb.com/pepsite/Camps/camps_index.html

This site gives a directory of computer camps all over the nation. If you love computers you may want to go to one of these camps and meet other kids who share that love. You can go to a day camp or a residence camp. Either way it will be a blast!

Shake Hands with Your Future
www.orgs.ttu.edu/IDEAL/shakehan.htm
This summer enrichment program is offered at Texas Tech University to students starting grades 4-11. Students can take classes that will teach them about careers in engineering, law, the arts, journalism, and many more. At this camp you can learn what you are passionate about and what kind of career would help you follow your passion. What a great way to spend your summer!

Girl Power Engineering Summer Science Camps
www.scifi.usask.ca/girlpower.html
This all-girl camp is aimed at teaching girls about science and technology. By the end of your time at the camp you will have a better understanding of how you fit into the growing technological and scientific world and what you can do to start a career in these exciting fields.

Summer Camp at the Virginia Air and Space Center
www.vasc.org/camp.html
The Virginia Air and Space Center offers a large selection of day camps and camp-ins for Girl and Boy Scouts. The camps are not just about astronomy. They feature many different types of science as well. You can create anything from stalactites to roller coasters (camps may vary from year to year). The age range for the day camps is 5 to 16.

Sally Ride Science Camps for Girls
www.sallyridecamps.com/ScienceCamp/
These overnight camps take place on college campuses in Atlanta, Georgia, and at Stanford University in California. Established by America's first woman in space, Sally Ride, these camps focus on astronomy and use college resources to look into the depths of space. These camps are for girls in grades 6-8.

AWSEM: Advocates for Women in Science, Engineering, and Mathematics

www.awsem.org

This site explains the mission of this organization, and how they are helping girls get more involved in science.

Bill Nye the Science Guy

www.nyelabs.com

Bill Nye's web site is a lot of fun for the science enthusiast. On this site you'll find fun experiments you can do at home, send silly e-cards, read about past episodes of the show, and find out more about the science guy himself.

Oregon Museum of Science and Industry (OMSI) Summer Camps

www.omsi.edu

OMSI offers some amazing hands-on camps in a variety of different fields that will get everyone excited and involved. The Pacific Ocean and the Cascade Mountains are only two of the wonderful natural resources in OMSI's backyard. Classes are for people of all ages, including adults and families.

The Junior Engineering Technical Society (JETS)

www.jets.org

This society is primarily for junior and senior high school students who want to get more involved in science and want to begin to prepare for college. You can participate in many contests or start your own science team to get involved. Some contests only require a computer; others are a lot more involved. You can choose which one suits you best and get started experimenting.

National Science Teachers' Association

www.nsta.org/students

This site is not just for teachers. You can also go to the students' area and learn about science contests, how energy works, and what it takes to be a science teacher. The site also has links to sites in many different fields of science so you can research different aspects for an experiment for one of their contests.

Summer Days: Math and Science Camps for Girls

www.mathandsciencecamp.com

These camps work to strengthen girls' self-confidence and interest in math and science. Campers learn about possible careers and how math and science apply to everyday life. The camp takes place at Echo Hill Outdoor school in Maryland. Girls are able to study specimens in their natural habitat and have a lot of fun at the same time.

Fun Science Web Sites

Oregon Museum of Science and Industry

www.omsi.edu/explore/online.cfm

Explore the amazing exhibits of the Oregon Museum of Science and Industry without leaving your house. On this Web site you can see how the human brain ages, hold your own paper plane competition, or see the latest images of the earth from space, along with many other great activities.

The Exploratorium

www.exploratorium.com

This site makes you feel like one of the elite few who know what is going on at the cutting edge of science. You can take a quiz about the science of cooking and get a video tour of the Scharffen Berger chocolate factory. There are loads of amazing experiments that you can do with the things laying around your house. What are you waiting for? Get experimenting!

Building Big

www.pbs.org/wgbh/buildingbig

You may have caught the TV special on PBS called "Building Big," but even if you didn't you can go to this Web site and learn what it is like to be an engineer. Not only can you read about some of the great structures of the world but you can also construct bridges and make decisions that professional engineers make every day.

Amazing Space

amazing-space.stsci.edu

On this site you can learn about gravity and velocity in space and use that knowledge to launch comets at Jupiter. You can also explore different galaxies with amazing pictures sent back from the Hubble space telescope and watch the aging of a star.

Women in Science

Women in Science

library.thinkquest.org/20117/

Here you can take a virtual walk through laboratories and learn about female scientists of today and yesterday. Maybe this Web site will encourage you to become a scientist of tomorrow. You can even personally contact the scientists and ask them about their research.

Women's History

womenshistory.about.com/library/bio/blbio_list_science.htm

This site contains biographies of all the heroines of science. If you have a scientific idol and you want to learn more about her, go to this site and read about her and others of her time.

Autodesk: Design Your Future

www.autodesk.com/dyf/dyfmain2.html

The best part of this site is that it is made by girls for girls. There are games and links to sites about science and women in the work force. It even has a comic strip!

Distinguished Women of Past and Present

www.distinguishedwomen.com/subject/field.html

If there is a famous women in a professional career that you have always wanted to know more about, this is your chance. This Web site has information on hundreds of women from many different backgrounds who have succeeded in their professions.

African Americans in Science

www.princeton.edu/~mcbrown/display/faces.html

This site pays tribute to the great contributions that African American men and women have given to their fields over the years.

4000 Years of Women in Science

www.astr.ua.edu/4000WS/summary.shtml

If our book left you wanting to learn more about all the other female scientists through time, visit this Web site and you can read their stories.

Women in Technology International

www.witi.com

There are women out there making new discoveries every day. This site will tell you all about their latest discoveries and what some of them are working on currently.

Women in World History

www.womeninworldhistory.com

They say that behind every great man is a woman. This Web site proves that this is true. It also shows that there are many women who made it on their own, not just in science, but in many fields.

National Women's History Project

http://www.nwhp.org

The National Women's History Project celebrates women throughout history who have made a difference. On this site you'll find information about Women's History Month and biographies of famous women in all fields, including science.

Science Sites

Grippy and Cormo's Science Activities

www.geocities.com/Broadway/1928/science_activities.htm

Grippy and Cormo have neat information on rocks, magnets, and water as well as a great site to help you get started on that science fair project. The site helps you ask all the right questions so you can get started in the right direction and don't have to start over five times.

How Stuff Works
www.howstuffworks.com
Are you constantly trying to pull apart the remote because you want to know how it transmits information to the TV? Then this Web site is for you. It shows you how to burn your own CD and much more.

Biomedia
ebiomedia.com/index.html
Learn about the tiny organisms that surround us and take the organism quiz. You can also participate in the creature contest. When you are done with all that you can browse through the incredible pictures they have all over their Web site.

United States Patent and Trademark Office: Kids Pages
www.uspto.gov/go/kids/kidprimer.html
Inventing is something that anyone can do. All you have to do is think about something that would be useful to you and your friends that has never been made and then make it. To make sure no one copies your idea you need to get a patent. You can find out how patents are used and how to go about applying for one on this site.

Sites for Girls

Equity Online
www.edc.org/WomensEquity
This Web site will keep you up to date on the latest news about women's rights and gender equality. It has a new fact every day to remind you of the state of the world and its women.

Terrifichick
www.terrifichick.com
Do you ever just need to vent about how your life is going? This is the Web

site for you. Girls can go to this site and post messages on the message board, or ask questions of fellow Terrifichicks. You can write your own book or movie reviews and read comments from other girls. Most of all, it is all about being yourself.

Girl Power
www.girlpower.gov
A Web site established by the U.S. Department of Health and Human Services to encourage girls just entering their teenage years to continue taking care of themselves. It has activities and a science and technology area where you can learn to design and make your own Web pages and where you can learn about careers in science.

A Girl's World
www.agirlsworld.com
A Girl's World has interviews with the hottest new celebrities and with everyday girls. It has a diary where girls can share their embarrassing experiences or learn from other people's difficulties. And, of course, it has games.

Educating Jane.com
www.educatingjane.com
Learn how to play mancala, do a crossword puzzle, all on Educating-Jane.com. This site includes a little bit of history, a little bit of theater, a little bit of everything! It will teach you how to do that one thing that you have always wanted to do but could never find instructions.

Sources

Adams, Richard and Robert Gardner. *Ideas for Science Projects*. Danbury,CT: Franklin Watts, 1997.

Adams, Richard C. and Robert Gardner. *More Ideas for Science Projects*, revised edition. New York / Danbury CT: Franklin Watts, 1998.

Altman, Linda Jacobs. *Women Inventors*. New York: Facts on File, Inc., 1997.

"Astronomical Society of the Pacific." www.astrosociety.org/index.html (20 December 2002).

Atkins, Jeannine. *Girls Who Looked Under Rocks: The Lives of Six Pioneering Naturalists*. Bt. Bound, 2001.

Baum, Joan. *The Calculating Passion of Ada Byron*. Hampden, CT: The Shoe String Press,1986.

"Biographies & Other Information." http://womenshistory.about.com/ (20 December 2002).

Bortz, Alfred. *To the Young Scientist*. New York: Franklin Watts, 1997.

Bottoone, Frank. *The Science of Life*. Chicago: The Chicago Review Press, 2001.

"C.J. Walker." http://www.princeton.edu/~mcbrown/display/walker.html (14 August 2003).

"Calling All Girls." http://geology.about.com/library/weekly/aa082700a.htm (20 August 2002).

"Carolyn Herschel." http://astro.berkeley.edu/~gmarcy/women/herschel.html (14 August 2003).

"Carolyn Herschel." http://ephemeris.sjaa.net/0205/c.html (30 April 2002).

"Carolyn Shoemaker." http://cannon.sfsu.edu/~gmarcy/cswa/history/shoemaker.html (14 August 2003).

Castner, James L. *Deep in the Amazon: Rainforest Researchers.* New York: Benchmark Books, 2002.

"Chien Shiung Wu." http://www.astr.ua.edu/4000WS/WU.html (5 June 2003).

"Constellations." http://www.emufarm.org/~cmbell/myth/myth.html (17 May 2002).

"Dian Fossey." http://www.gorillas.org/ (21 June 2002).

"Dorothy Crowfoot Hodgkin." http://almaz.com/nobel/chemistry/dch.html (14 February 2003).

"Elizabeth Blackwell." http://www.astr.ua.edu/4000WS/BLACKWELL.html (15 May 2003).

"Elizabeth Blackwell." http://www.nlm.nih.gov/hmd/blackwell/ (21 June 2002).

"Elizabeth Britton." http://womenshistory.about.com/library/bio/blbio_britton_elizabeth.htm (15 June 2003).

"Ellen Swallow Richards Residence." http://www.cr.nps.gov/nr/travel/ pwwmh/ma67.htm (14 August 2003).

"Ellen Swallow Richards." http://curie.che.virginia.edu/scientist/ 1 richards.html (25 September2002).

Fasulo, Michael and Paul Walker. *Careers in the Environment.* Chicago: VGM Career Horizons, 2000.

"Florence Nightengale." http://www.bbc.co.uk/education/medicine/ nonint/indust/ht/inhtbi1.shtml (18 March 2003).

"Frances Kelsey." http://americanhistory.si.edu/hosc/molecule/05drug.htm (17 December 2002).

Gabor, Andrea. *Einstein's Wife: Work and Marriage in the Lives of Five Great Twentieth-Century Women.* New York: Penguin Books, 1995.

"How Women Make Science Work." http://www.wired.com/news/ technology/0,1282,40757,00.html (20 August 2002).

"Distinguished Women." http://www.distinguishedwomen.com/ biographies/richards-es.html(14 August 2003).

Ingram, Jay. *The Barmaid's Brain and Other Strange Tales from Science.* New York: WH Freeman & Co., 1998.

"International Astronomical Union." http://www.iau.org/ (20 December 2002).

"Irène Joliot-Curie." http://www.woodrow.org/teachers/chemistry/ institutes/1992/IreneJoliot-Curie.html (15 August 2002).

"It's a Woman's Invention." http://www.cafezine.com/index_article.asp? deptid=2&id=159 (14 August 2003).

Jemison, Dr. Mae. *Find Where the Wind Goes: Moments from My Life*. New York: Scholastic Press, 2001.

"Joan Feynman." http://www.popsci.com/popsci/science/article/ 0,12543,231816,00.html (13 May 2003).

"Josephine Cochrane." http://www.girltech.com/Invention/IN%5 Finvention%5Fintro.html(14 November 2002).

Kahn, Jetty. *Women in Computer Science Careers*. Mankato, MN: Capstone Press, 2000.

Karnes, Frances A. and Suzanne M. Bean. *Girls and Young Women Inventing*. Minneapolis: Free Spirit Publishing, Inc., 1995.

Kelsey, Jane. *Science: VGM's Career Portraits*. Chicago: VGM Career Horizons, 1997.

"Lady Mary Wortley Montague." http://www.fordham.edu/halsall/mod/ montagu-smallpox.html (13 July 2003).

"Lady Mary Wortley Montague." http://www.bbc.co.uk/education/ medicine/nonint/indust/dt/indtbi1.shtml (2 July 2002).

Lambert, Lisa A. *The Leakeys*. Vero Beach, FL: Rourke Publications, 1993.

Lear, Linda. *Rachel Carson: Witness for Nature*. Henry Holt & Co.: New York, 1997.

Macdonald, Anne L. *Feminine Ingenuity: Women and Invention in America*. Ballantine: New York, 1992.

"Margaret Burbidge." http://astro.berkeley.edu/~gmarcy/women/ burbidge.html (14 August2003).

"Maria Mitchell." http://womenshistory.about.com/library/ bio/blbio_mitchell_maria.htm(21 June 2003).

Marson, Ron, with Peg Marson and Don Balick. *Global TOPS: 100 Science Lessons With 15 Simple Things*, Teacher Resource Manual. Canby, OR: TOPS Learning Systems, 1998.

"Mary Anning." http://www.dinosaur.org/dinotimemachine.htm (8 August 2003).

"Mary Leakey." http://www.strangescience.net/leakey.htm (7 June 2003).

"Mary Seacole." http://www.bbc.co.uk/education/medicine/nonint/ indust/dt/indtbi3.shtml (23 April 2003).

Maze Productions. *I Want to be an Engineer*. New York: Harcourt Brace & Co., 1997.

McGrayne, Sharon Bertsch. *Nobel Prize Women in Science*. New York: Birch Lane Press, 1993.

McGrayne, Sharon Bertsch. *Nobel Prize Women in Science*, Second Edition. Washington D.C.: Joseph Henry Press, 2001.

Moje, Steven. *Cool Chemistry*. New York: Sterling Publishing, 1999.

Morell, Virginia. *Ancestral Passions: The Leakey Family and the Quest for Humankind's Beginnings*. New York: Simon and Schuster, 1995.

Mowat, Farley. *Woman in the Mists: The Story of Dian Fossey and the Mountain Gorillas of Africa*. New York: Warner Books, Inc., 1987.

Nelson, Bob. "Famed Physicist Chien-Shiung Wu Dies at 84," Columbia University Record, Vol. 22, No. 15. February 21,1997.

"Nobel Prize Women in Science." http://books.nap.edu/books/03090
72700/html/index.html (15 August 2002).

"Observation of Stars." http://plato.phy.ohiou.edu/~dutta/
notes/node9.html (23 January2003).

Pasternak, Ceel. *Cool Careers for Girls as Environmentalists*. Manassas Park,
VA: Impact Publications, 2002.

Poynter, Margaret. *The Leakeys: Uncovering the Origins of Humankind*.
Springfield, NJ: Enslow Publishers, Inc., 1997.

"Rachel Carson." http://www.ecotopia.org/ehof/carson/ (21 May 2002).

"Rachel Carson." http://www.lkwdpl.org/wihohio/cars-rac.htm (21 June
2003).

"Rachel Carson." http://www.time.com/time/time100/scientist/profile/
carson.html (5May 2002).

Rayner-Canham, Marelene & Geoffrey. *Women in Chemistry*. Philadelphia,
PA: Chemical Heritage Foundation, 2001.

Reeves, Diane Lindsey. *Career Ideas for Kids Who Like Science*. New York:
Checkmark Books, 1998.

Sacks, Oliver. *Uncle Tungsten: Memories of a Chemical Boyhood*. New York:
Random House, 2001.

"Sarah Whiting." http://www.physics.ucla.edu/~cwp/Phase2/
Whiting,_Sarah_Frances@944123456.html (14 August 2003).

"Scoping out Women." http://ephemeris.sjaa.net/0205/c.html
(30 April 2002).

Sobey, Ed. *Inventing Stuff.* Palo Alto, CA: Dale Seymour Publications, 1996.

Stein, Dorothy. *Ada: A Life and a Legacy.* Cambridge: MIT Press, 1985.

Stille, Darlene R. *Extraordinary Women Scientists.* Chicago: Children's Press, 1995.

Sullivan, Otha Richard. *African American Women Scientists and Inventors.* New York: John Wiley & Sons, Inc., 2002.

"The Moon Goddess." http://exn.ca/apollo/Moon/ (14 August 2003).

"The Nobel E-Museum." http://www.nobel.se (15 August 2002).

"The Weeping God." http://www.mayalords.org/incfldr/moon.html (14 June 2002).

"The Woodrow Wilson Fellowship Foundation." http://www.woodrow.org (23 July 2003).

Thimmesh, Catherine. *Girls Think of Everything.* New York: Houghton Mifflin Company, 2000.

Trefil, James S. *The Edge of the Unknown: 101 Things You Don't Know About Science and No One Else Does, Either.* Houghton Mifflin, Co., 1996.

Vare, Ethlie Ann and Greg Ptacek. *Mothers of Invention.* New York: William Morrow and Company, 1988.

Vare, Ethlie Ann and Greg Ptacek. *Patently Female.* New York: John Wiley and Sons, Inc., 2002.

Wiggers, Raymond. *The Amateur Geologist.* New York: Franklin Watts, 1993.

"Women in Astronomy." http://www.astro.helsinki.fi/~eisaksso/ heaven.html (14 August 2003).

"Women in Paleontology." http://www.strangescience.net/women.htm (14 August 2002).

Acknowledgements

The authors would like to thank all the folks who gave their support and encouragement to this project, including our family and friends, the staff at Beyond Words Publishing Inc. and the Oregon Museum of Science and Industry (OMSI). Thanks to all the young women who answered our call for essays on the joys of science, and the patient young "research teams" who enthusiastically reviewed as much of our material as they could before bedtime.

We would like especially to mention Marilyn Johnson, Karen Kane, Craig Reed, Anders Liljeholm, Ellie Caldwell, Nicole Stencel, Theresa Mau, Olivia Westfall, and Sue Wu, Amy Odman, Kate, Ruth, Nan, Olivia, and friends. Thank you to Robert Barnett, Nora Coon, Kristen Getz, Kristin Hilton, Elisa Libiran, Madeline Maxwell, Brenda Smith, and Whitney Quon for all your hard work.

Also, thank you to Debbie Palen for her wonderful illustrations that really bring the book to life.

About the Authors

Erica Ritter has worked at the Oregon Museum of Science and Industry (OMSI) since 1999, sharing amazing science with visitors of all ages. Some of her favorite projects include overnight science camp-ins, curriculum development, teacher workshops, and contributing to the museum's First Aid, Sustainability, and Latinas en Ciencia programs. Erica's office is in the OMSI Chemistry Lab, where she works with visitors and cooks up new hands-on chemistry activities like the "Chemistry of Food" and "Chemistry of Art."

Beth Caldwell Hoyt is a publicist for Beyond Words Publishing, which has published such young adult favorites as *Girls Who Rocked the World, Girls Know Best* and *The Girls' Life Guide to Growing Up*. She has been a writer and editor for various newspapers and the technical magazine *MCP* (*Microsoft Certified Professional*). Beth is a graduate of Scripps College and an avid fan of Bill Nye "The Science Guy."

Erica and Beth both reside in Portland, Oregon.